E.B. BROWN

GHOST DANCE

A NOVEL

BLUE DOG PRESS
NEW JERSEY

D1522190

Ghost Dance
Copyright © 2016 by E.B. Brown
All rights reserved.

Published in the United States by Blue Dog Press LLC, New Jersey

For information:
http://www.ebbrown.net

ALSO BY E.B. BROWN

The Legend of the Bloodstone

Return of the Pale Feather

Of Vice and Virtue

A Tale of Oak and Mistletoe

Time Walkers The Complete Collection

The Big Book of Time Travel Romance

Time Rift

Time Game

Time Over

The Viking Sagas Collection

Time Song

The Seventh Key

The Fifth Key

The Ninth Key

The Pretenders Complete Collection

Ghost Dance

Season of Exile

Roam: Time Walkers World Special Edition

The Replacement 1

The Replacement 2

The Replacement 3

Writing as Ellis Brown

Jack Made Me Do It

CONTENTS

If you can change the truth of your past
And choose what should begin and what should never be
Tell me, now, how one might wield that power
Or how it might be meant for one man's whim

– Cockacoeske, Queen of the Pamunkey 1656

PROLOGUE

The Battle of Bloody Run
James River Falls, 1656
Daniel

HAD HE KNOWN what was to come, would he still have traveled that same path? Not only for knowing that it *would* end, as all lives do, but for the when and how of it? For truth, it was a tricky question since he was privy to the history of time before it happened, yet despite that unfair advantage, Daniel knew the answer in his heart.

Yes.

Even as his face pressed into the cold sodden earth and he tasted the muddy grit on his tongue, his answer remained unchanged. The trickle of warm blood seeping into the corner of his eye would not sway him, nor the scent of his enemy's rancid breath upon his cheek.

Yes. I would do it again, he thought. *For what am I, if not a spawn of two worlds, a man beholden at once to all and to none?*

Blows from a club rained down on his back, taking the last of the breath from his lungs. Beneath his ribs, down deep in his belly, his muscles spasmed, and he could no longer draw air when he gasped. He could not see his enemy but he could still feel the presence of the man with the club, and although the attack had ceased, Daniel knew there was little time to catch his breath before it would resume.

Totopotomoi – the Pamunkey Chief – was dead. Their English allies deserted them like cowards, fleeing from the battlefield as the bodies of Pamunkey warriors fell to the muddy earth. Had Colonel Hill and his Colonial Militia ever meant to stand beside the Pamunkey, or was it his plan all along to run, leaving the Pamunkey to fight the Ricahecrians alone?

It no longer mattered. The Ricahecrian with the club standing above him would not spare him, and Daniel knew he would soon join his companions.

"Is he dead?" one of his enemies asked.

Daniel winced when the tip of a foot jabbed into his ribs.

"Not yet," another man answered. "Leave him. This is the one *Wicawa Ni Tu* wants. Let our War Chief have the honor of ending his life."

The men laughed to each other as they walked away, their voices echoing through Daniel's skull and pounding in his ears. When he was certain they were gone, he buried his fingers in the damp ground and moved to raise his head. With all the damage done to his body it was no easy task, and it took a few moments before he could lift himself enough to look around.

By the tears of the Creator, he had never seen such a sight. Was this the *Hell* the Christian Englishmen spoke of? Only a few paces to his side lay dozens of fallen Pamunkey braves. Limbs were twisted, heads bloodied. A man Daniel had stood with at Colonel Hill's side was propped up, run through with a spear that impaled him to the tree at his back. A lanyard of eagle feathers around his neck fluttered in the wisp of a breeze, tangled in long dark strands of the warrior's hair. Daniel did not want to look at him, yet he could not look away. The man's eyes stared straight ahead, an empty chasm, and for a moment Daniel swore his dead lips moved.

"*Run,*" the dead man whispered. "*Hurry.*"

So he did. Daniel forced the remnants of his strength into his limbs, clawing at the dirt until he started to move. He darted a glance over the bodies of the dead and saw no enemy near, yet he could hear them in the distance and he knew they would return for him. When he gathered enough purchase to rise, he crouched on one knee with his hand over his belly, the burning taste of bile searing his throat. The river was close; he could smell the dampness in the air and hear the rush of the water nearby.

It called to him, and he obeyed.

A Ricahecrian bellowed a joyful war cry, and it was then that Daniel knew he was the last one left alive. He scrambled down the steep sandy bank and slid into the cold water, stumbling through the shallow stream bed until he reached a deeper spot. He tried to steady himself but when he waded deeper the force of the current struck him like a barrel in the chest, and for a long moment he clutched the slippery root of a tree.

Death was assured if he stayed, yet fleeing could give him no certainty of survival. The sounds of war cries echoing through the trees drew closer and Daniel looked down at his fingers entwined in the tree root.

He let go.

The frigid water took what was left of him, welcoming him, and he did not object this time as the current pulled him away from shore.

It was not long before numbness settled deep into his bones. Even in his dreams, he had never felt so peaceful, so weightless. The gentle lapping of the current rocked him and washed over his wounds, licking them clean and taking away his pain.

If this is the afterlife, he thought, *then perhaps I have nothing to fear.*

Every few moments he reminded himself to raise his head and open his mouth, taking a breath of air into his bruised lungs as he was carried downstream. A part of him realized he could not stay submerged for too long and that he must make an effort to float, but another part of him wished to simply give in. *Let the water take me, wherever I am meant to be.*

Water flowed over his open mouth and filled his lungs. He choked it up by pure reflex, past caring to fight it any longer. In the murky depths of his scattered thoughts, visions of his fallen companions spoke to him, taunting him as he drifted farther away from the carnage. He could hear the voices of the dead call to him over the sound of his own ragged breaths.

"Go," the ghosts commanded. *"Live!"*

He listened to them as best he could until the current slowed and his legs found purchase in shallow water once more. Although he much preferred to remain floating, the Creator had a different plan for him. It was with that assurance that he left the water and made his way onto a quiet sandy bank where the only sign of life was a pair of spotted-back turtles resting on a patch of tuckahoe. Loose pebbles shifted beneath him when he

10

crawled out of the creek and he felt the quick rush of a cold breeze take the air from his lungs as he gasped and coughed.

The panicked cries of sand gulls protested his intrusion and he could hear the flutter of their wings above him in the trees. His breath left him in a groan as he pushed himself up on one arm. He stilled for a moment, cocking his head slightly to the side. He was not yet too far gone to ignore the new sound coming towards him, the creeping echo of something walking through the brush that he was certain was no animal.

Yet when he raised his eyes and the last glimmers of amber rays from the fading sunset blinded him, the shadowed outline of a woman breached his weary sight. There, in front of him, she stood like a messenger from the Creator, her illuminated form taking the very breath from his tired chest.

Daniel squinted, raising his hand to shield his gaze. Was this the one meant to take him from this time, sent to guide him on his final path? She was not as he expected. Not with her honey-colored hair streaming free over her shoulders, nor with her pale face defined by the glow of the setting sun. She was dressed in a peculiar manner with her legs covered with some sort of tight trouser, and he could see heavy leather boots the color of doe skin on her feet. Perhaps the Christians were right about death, and this was one of their angels sent to gather his soul. He shook his head as if the motion might clear his vision, but when he opened his eyes again and she remained, he knew what to he must do.

He reached for her, his hand slipping down past her trousers to settle around one bared ankle.

"Take me home," he said, his voice hoarse. "I am ready now."

Instead of the comforting embrace he expected, she leaned forward and peered down at him. In her hands was an odd shaped flintlock pistol, smaller than those the English used, and as she raised it up in her fisted hand he wondered why a spirit guide might have need of such a weapon.

"Christ!" she hissed. "Not today. I am *not* doing this bullshit today!"

He had no time to wonder over her strange reply before she struck him with the weapon, smashing it into the side of his head. Darkness exploded around him. His hold on her ankle slipped away, and he sighed as the blessed sanctuary of the afterlife swallowed him whole.

1

Philadelphia, 2014
Emmy

THE WAIL OF a car horn was too late to warn Emmy that she stepped off the curb too soon. It was her own fault for fumbling with her ringing cell phone while trying to maneuver through city traffic, but when the splash of muddy sewer runoff soaked her new suede ankle boots and the phone in her hand continued to ring, she answered the call with a none-too-polite curse.

"Damn it, Connor, I'm walking into the building now!" she said. "What is so important that you couldn't wait five minutes?" It was her brother, and she was literally ten feet away from the back entrance of the hospital where they both worked. She was fairly sure that he could see her from the window of his cushy physician's office above the emergency department. He was probably just calling to bust her stones for being late, but with the way her hangover was ringing through her ears, she was in no mood for his older brother nonsense.

"Emmy – it's Derek. Where are you?"

She paused mid-stride, one foot on the first step to the entrance. *Why was her brother's best friend calling her from Connor's phone?* She tucked a wayward strand of her long hair behind her ear, feeling the cool nip of early autumn wind race down her spine, but it was not the weather that chilled her the most. Sirens echoed around her, swallowing the city noise as she took in the spectacle around her. Chaos did not usually stir her; after all, she had been working in the city hospital in some capacity or another since she'd been a teenager. Yet there was nothing ordinary about the edge of panic in Derek's voice, nor the half-dozen police cars swarmed together at the emergency department entrance.

"I'm at the door," she explained, stumbling over her words. "I – I'm just running late. I was out with friends last night."

"Stay right there. I'm coming to get you," he replied.

The automatic slider opened in front of her. Up ahead in the long corridor she spotted Derek walking briskly towards her, pulling the phone from his ear when their eyes met. She dropped her hand and shoved her phone into her back pocket, aware her hands were shaking.

Derek was dressed casually in jeans and a polo shirt instead of his typical police sergeant's gear, flanked by two uniformed patrol officers. As he drew closer she realized his upper arm was wrapped with a fresh bandage – and that a round circle of bright red blood was seeping through it.

"What's going on?" she asked. "What happened to you? Why did you call me from Connor's phone?"

He waved off the two officers beside him and placed his hand on her shoulder, his fingers gripping her as if he meant to steady himself more than her. She could see his throat tighten and he swallowed before he spoke, his words coming out in a low rush.

"It's Connor. God, Emmy, I'm so sorry..."

Derek's demeanor crumbled, his eyes rimmed red with tears.

She shook her head, unwilling to hear the rest of what Derek needed to say. "Where is he?"

"We – we went to lunch, and I was dropping him off here ... we stopped to help a stranded motorist," he said, his voice hoarse. "It was a scam. They started shooting when they saw my badge –"

"No," Emmy whispered. She suspected what he was going to say next, but if she denied it out loud then it was almost as if she could deny it was true.

"He's gone, Emmy. He's dead."

She jerked her arm away from him. The sharp reflex was stronger than any sense of rational behavior at that moment as she stared at the man she considered an adoptive brother. Seeing tears stream down his strong face sent her into a spiral, crushing what was left of her control.

"Where is he?" she demanded. "Tell me where is! I want to see him!"

When Derek reached for her, she s′ backward, searching the sad gazes in the crowd ′ gathered around them. She knew every face, a coworkers and friends she had known for ye working as Connor's clerk. One of the womer take her hand and Emmy moved back agains′ tile wall to get away from the comforting touch. not lose herself in the luxury of grief, nor afford to fall apart when she knew what she ha

There was no time to waste. She needed to see Connor, and she needed to see him now – before it was too late to make a difference.

"Tell me where he is, Derek," she said, forcing the words through her tight lips. "Please," she added.

He nodded and held his hand out towards the trauma room, ushering her ahead without touching her. She regretted her cold behavior but she would regret it even more if she wasted one more moment in a show of mourning. Derek tried to follow her inside, but she closed the door in his face.

There could be no witness to what she meant to do.

For all of her life she was trained to heal, yet for Emmy the act of healing was much more than what modern medicine could accomplish. She slipped her hand beneath the edge of her jacket and felt for the leather lanyard around her neck. Hanging snug against her skin was the glass ampule, and it was with a shaking hand that she raised it to eye level.

Yes, she thought. It wasn't his time to die; Connor was meant for greater things. All the plans they had made, all the sacrifices they had endured, it would all be for nothing if his heart did not start beating once more. Surely, this is what mother meant when she told Emmy here would be one chance to use the contents of the vial.

"I'm going to do it," she said, more to herself than Connor. Could he hear her speak while he was ⸳ering in that in-between chasm of light and ⸱ness? Perhaps he was already swallowed by the ⸳ side and it would make no difference. Still, she had

She snapped the top of the ampule and grimaced the glass pierced her thumb. *No matter.* The

16

ampule was filled with her own crimson blood, gathered from her heel by her mother when Emmy was a newborn. A dash of old mixed with the new should make no difference.

Emmy pulled back the white sheet that covered Connor, exposing the wound that ended his life. She ignored the sudden rush of déjà vu when she looked down at him, passing it off as just a byproduct of her frazzled state, taking a moment to let the strange feeling pass so that she could move on to what she needed to do.

It was a gunshot to the chest, directly over his heart, covered only by a piece of fresh loose gauze. She imagined it was just a courtesy gesture since the staff knew she would want to see him and it would hardly do to have a blood stain seeping through on the sheet. As she clutched the vial in her hand and stared down at the silly piece of gauze, a hysterical laugh bubbled in her throat.

It was senseless and sad at the same time. Seeing her dead brother on the table was enough to pierce her sanity. Yet knowing what she was about to do was something out of a twisted fairytale.

Biting down hard on her lower lip to keep steady, Emmy brushed the gauze off the wound. It was just as horrific as she suspected, and she tried not to look at it as she dumped the contents of the ampule onto the jagged mess of skin that once covered Connor's heart.

When it was done she stepped slowly backward. The remnants of the ampule dropped from her hand, shattering on the tile floor at her feet. She could not bear to watch it happen, yet she could not tear her eyes away once his flesh started to mend. Nipping and stretching, jagged edges merging together, it was as if tiny needles jabbed at his chest while the breath of life surged back into his body. Connor's ribcage expanded, nearly pulling him upward off the gurney, but then a gentle unseen force eased him down. Over and over his lungs filled and emptied, breathing but not breathing as his broken body healed from inside out.

The gravity of what it meant suddenly crashed down on her. *All the stories mother told them were true.* All those years Emmy spent listening to her tales, fearing that her mother was stone-cold crazy. After all, it was the twenty-first century and people didn't run around with magical vials of blood hanging around their necks. Emmy always looked at the tiny ampule with respect, as if it was an old family heirloom, but the enormity of that power hit her full on like a punch to the gut.

Mother was right. Emmy's blood could heal the dead.

And it was healing her dead brother.

Connor's eyes fluttered open. He said nothing at first, his gaze traveling warily from the ceiling down towards his chest. When his eyes met hers, she thought she might burst if he was anything other than the brother she loved.

"Emmy," he whispered. "What did you do?"

Her throat tightened. "I saved you."

"You used your blood."

His response was more of a statement than anything, his accusation hanging heavy in the air between them. She nodded, staring back at him with the best defiant glare she could muster considering the sheer insanity of the situation.

Connor was dead. Then she poured her newborn blood on him, and he stopped being dead. Mother did not lie when she explained the history of their ancestors, of all those that had the sacred blood in their veins. Although she grew up with the knowledge practically hammered into her daily by her mother and she knew what she was born to do, Emmy had never expected to have to make the choice alone. It wasn't something one could truly grasp in the span of a few moments, nor something she might ever believe was real if she had not seen it happen before her own eyes – and by her own hand.

"I'd do it again," she said.

Connor uttered a sigh. With a shockingly swift motion he sat up on the gurney, dropping his long bare legs over the edge to dangle. One hand drifted to his chest, where he clutched his newly mended skin for a long moment.

"We have to go. I know you did what you thought you had to do, but this changes our plans," he said. He shifted his weight and stood up, the slap of his bare feet on the tile floor echoing through the dimly lit room. She didn't miss the edge of frustration in his voice.

"We can go somewhere else. Start over. Like we did before –"

"It's too late for that now and you know it. It's time for us to go. We can't put it off any longer," Connor replied.

Emmy took a pair of scrub bottoms from the linen cart in the corner and handed them to Connor, numb with the reality of events set in motion. No, she would not change what she had done, and a part of her was glad she had not considered the aftermath of her choice

19

when she broke open the ampule. If Connor was hell-bent on making her leave the only true home she had ever known, well, then he was damn well going to travel with her.

"Fine. You're going to have to go out the rear service door. I'll distract everyone out front as long as I can," she said. "I'll meet you back at the house. My bag is in the back of my closet. I assume you're packed?"

"Of course I'm packed," he said, his voice tinged with annoyance. "I've been ready, Emmy. You've just forced our hand with this stunt." He ran his hand through his thick blond hair, shaking his head with a bit of a wince. Dried blood flaked off his skin as he moved. Emmy briefly wondered if he had any pain from his injury, but there was no time to delve into a game of twenty questions when they had to figure out how to get his creepy undead ass out of the hospital without being caught.

"Like I'd let you die and leave me to figure this out all alone!" Emmy shot back.

"Nice," he muttered. "But thank you." He planted a quick kiss on her forehead and she smiled, biting back a harsh retort. He was definitely behaving like his old self, so that was enough to calm her in light of all that had happened.

With a last glance at her and a flash of a surly grin, Connor went towards the rear service entrance. The weight of it all seemed to smother her, lapping at her restraint with each breath she took to steady herself. But she reminded herself she was made of stronger stuff, and this was not the time to lose her marbles. The harsh resolution was enough to drive her forward and she turned around and steeled herself to face the crowd of people outside the room, slamming directly into Derek's chest in the process.

"W-what the hell is going on?" Derek stammered, grabbing Emmy by the shoulders. *"Connor?"*

Connor paused, perched half-way out through the swinging rear door. He pivoted slowly, his shoulders tensed.

"Derek –" Emmy stammered. She looked helplessly at Connor, at a loss for anything sensible to say. When Connor turned fully around and faced them she thought Derek was going to pass out. The color drained from his skin and she could see the perspiration stand out on his face. Along his neck Emmy could see his veins tighten like the string of a bow, and it was all she could do to hold onto him when he tried to brush past her.

"You – you were dead. I *saw* you. Dead. Dead on that table!" Derek said, his voice cracking. He did not try to get closer to Connor again, allowing her a moment to get his attention.

"Listen to me," she demanded. She placed one hand flat on his chest and the other gently on his face, turning his chin with her thumb so that he had to look straight at her. "Derek, you *have* to listen to me. We don't have much time. We can't stay here."

Derek seemed to focus on her for a moment. His wild eyes met hers and she nodded.

"Your pendant is missing. The one with the vial," Derek said. His voice was somewhat calmer when he spoke as if suddenly he was arranging the pieces of a puzzle into a reasonable pattern. "So it's true. Your mother wasn't crazy."

"No, she wasn't," Connor interrupted, placing a hand on Derek's shoulder. "And we can't stay here any

21

longer. Are you done losing your shit yet? 'Cause we could really use your help."

Derek flinched and switched his gaze to Connor's chest.

"It really healed you? Her blood fixed it, just like – like that?" Derek replied.

"Yeah. Just like that," Connor agreed.

Emmy held her breath while the two best friends stared at each other. Although Derek had been privy to many of the Cameron family discussions, Emmy was not aware that he knew what the blood could do. Derek spent so much time at their home throughout the years that it was impossible for him to miss how insane their mother was, especially towards the end, but even so, it unnerved her. Some kind of unspoken agreement was reached between Derek and Connor in that long moment, leaving Emmy feeling as if she had missed a crucial detail.

"Then you two need to get out of here," Derek said. "Connor, you go out the back. I'll take Emmy home. We need to hurry. I can stall them, but they're going to notice the missing body by shift change if it doesn't end up in the morgue."

Derek and Connor clasped hands.

"Thank you, brother," Connor said. Derek nodded. The color was restored to his face and he seemed to shake off the insanity of the situation. Emmy wondered exactly how much Derek knew about their family secret, especially since Connor had always said to trust no one. The time to ask questions was rapidly diminishing and none of it would matter soon anyway.

It was time to leave. She couldn't bury the frustration seeping in, taunting her with the truth. If she had only left with Connor months ago, none of this would be happening. Connor would not have been shot, and she would still have her ampule lying safely from the lanyard around her neck.

Connor left them with a promise to meet at the house. Derek fell back into some semblance of normality, taking her hand in his and hauling her out of the trauma room.

The crowd of faces was a blur. She vaguely heard Derek say something about taking her home, and adding in some claim that Connor's body was sent to the morgue via the rear corridor.

He was right; they did not have much time. They'd notice the missing body, and then they would be coming straight to her door asking questions.

They drove together without speaking for the first few blocks. It was not a long ride, for which Emmy was grateful, but it was still long enough to punctuate an uncomfortable silence. As the familiar buildings whizzed by and dusk lowered down over the city, Emmy brushed the wetness from her eye with the edge of her clenched fist.

All she had ever known and loved would soon be only a bittersweet memory. She wondered who would visit mother's grave when they were gone. Emmy had no family save for Connor and Derek, and her friends were not the sentimental sort.

Derek pulled his car into the driveway of the house and turned off the engine. She reached for his hand as he was taking the keys from the ignition.

"I know you never really liked my mother," she said, "so I understand if you say no. It would just mean a lot to me if you would put flowers on her grave sometimes. Maybe on Mother's Day or something. Just so someone remembers her."

The line of his jaw tightened and looked sideways at her, his blue eyes shadowed.

"Of course I'll do that," he replied. "But what will I have to remember you by?" He took her hand and clutched it firmly in his own. She could feel him shaking and suddenly the way he stared at her seemed based on anything but brotherly affection. She did not know how to respond, so she slipped her arms around his neck and hugged him fiercely.

"I'm sorry," she whispered. "I wish – I wish you could go with us."

He sighed with a sad smile. "Yeah, well, that's not how this whole destiny thing works. We all have our part to play."

She drew back, letting him wipe the tears from her eyes. His grin faded when he looked at her, a shadow of hardness settling on his face as she considered the truth of his words.

"C'mon," he said, his voice hoarse. "Let's get you on your way."

Emmy followed him to the house. Tracing her fingers over the peeling paint on the front porch rail, she felt it crumble away at her touch. Was time and destiny layered the same way? A solid base with a fragile shield, waiting for just the right moment to turn into dust?

Next to the front door was her grey backpack. Connor was ready for them, dressed in fresh clothes and the emanating the picture of perfect health. In spite of all the chaos, his image gave her a sense of pride. Connor was alive because of the blood in her veins, and she would never regret saving him no matter what happened next.

"You'd better sit down for this," Connor instructed. Emmy nodded mutely, taking a seat on the edge of an ottoman. Connor dropped to one knee in front of her and took her hand into his, turning the palm upwards and splaying her fingers wide. Emmy let out a nervous chuckle when she saw the Sharpie marker he held, but by the scowl on his face she immediately realized he was serious.

"You can't mark me with *that!*" she said, pulling her hand back.

"Of course I can. It doesn't matter *how* the mark gets there – just that it's on your hand!" Connor shot back. When he snatched her hand again, she curled her fingers into a fist.

"No," she said. "Do it the right way. The way our mother taught you. With the knife." Emmy knew what she was asking of him, and she knew it would be difficult for him to do. It wasn't every day that a brother needed to carve a rune mark into his sister's hand, but they had no time for mistakes and Emmy was afraid of messing with the Old Ways too much.

"Emmy, no," he protested.

"Just do it. Stop being an idiot. If we're going to do this – if we're really going to do it – then I want to do it right. I don't want to end up in the wrong place. And I don't ever recall mother saying you could just draw the rune on my hand with a Sharpie. She said you have to carve it with a knife. So stop being a sissy and just do it."

Connor muttered a curse that she could not decipher and reached for his pack. When he drew the antique dagger from the side pocket, Derek stepped forward and grabbed his wrist.

"Wait a second! Is this the only way? There must be something else you can do," Derek insisted.

"'Fraid not. You heard her. She's probably right. We don't want to screw this up. Might as well just do it the right way," Connor replied.

Emmy thrust her hand forward in offering to her brother, squeezing her eyes shut. As much as she thought she was prepared for the pain, it still made her squirm and try to pull away. She fought back a spray of unwanted tears, reflexive products of the slicing of her skin. Thankfully, Derek put his arm around her shoulders and held her still while Connor worked, and in a blessed few seconds it was over. With one eye slightly open, she peered down at the bloody rune mark carved into her left hand.

"That's it?" she asked. "That's the First Mark?"

"Yeah. Some called it the First Key, but yeah, that's it. Now put it on me," he replied, handing her the knife. She looked down at the weapon, the weight of it heavy in her unmarked right hand. Embedded in the hilt was a green-black bloodstone with threadlike red streaks running through it, the ancient dagger that had once belonged to their father. With a quick look at her own palm for reference, she committed the image to memory and went to work on Connor's palm.

He was not as squeamish as she was, and it did not take her long to finish. Derek surveyed them in silence, his eyes wide and near panicked when Connor once again rifled through his pack. Emmy slid the straps of her grey sport backpack over her shoulders and tightened it, taking care to let the blood run freely from her new wound until Connor placed the Bloodstone pendant around her neck.

"If we are lost to each other, never let anyone see that stone. Keep it hidden, and trust no one. Any man can be corrupted when faced with the power you have in your blood."

"We won't be parted," she argued. Connor would have no part in her defiance, however, and he grasped her hand firmly in response.

"The First Mark is more dangerous than the others. It sends you to where you are meant to be, but it may not be the same place for both of us. I know where you will go. *My* place in all of this is not so certain. So promise me you'll stay safe," he demanded.

"Fine. Of course. I promise," she replied. She didn't like the idea of using the First Mark any more than he did, but there was no other option for them. They were hardly experts; all they had to go on was what they learned from their mother.

Connor nodded to Derek and adjusted Emmy's hand so that their fingers were tightly entwined. With his other hand, he gripped the hilt of the bloodstone dagger, and she knew it was time.

"Goodbye, Derek," she whispered.

The ground shuddered beneath her feet when she placed her bleeding palm over the bloodstone pendant hanging from her neck. The stone seared her flesh, bonding with the fresh blood that would leave a scar on her hand the same as her mother and brother had. At first, Connor's grip seemed to steady her in place, but the security of that bond quickly vanished once darkness swallowed her senses. The force of the travel was too much to bear, for any person to withstand, and when the wave hit her she thrust her hands over her ears and clutched her own head, begging the merciless pressure to stop.

It was a relentless thing, pulling her down deep into an abyss without end, until she gave it surrender and let her body sink down to the floor. Then, only then, with her face pressed to the cold tile, did she dare to take a breath, and she gave in to the glorious pull of unconsciousness.

When she woke, it was raw earth she felt on her cheek. Loose dirt crusted her skin and she could feel the sting of her wounded hand as she pulled herself up onto her knees and promptly vomited.

"Emmy?"

She turned her head slightly, still not quite done with the spasms in her stomach. Relief washed over her when she saw Connor lying on the ground a few feet away. He was flat on his back, blessedly safe and whole, and most importantly, he was there with her.

"We made it," she replied. Exactly *where* they made it to remained to be seen, but for now it was enough to know they would face it together.

Above them, a flock of black birds surged across the sky, rustling the trees with their sudden flight. A coating of sweet pine needle sap stained her hands, mixed in with the crusted blood, and she winced at the strong scent when she rubbed it off on her flannel shirt. She could hear the roar of rushing water nearby, and as she sat up and let her pack fall half-skewed off one shoulder, Connor rolled over and scrambled to his feet.

"My pack is missing," Connor said. He ran his hands through his thick blond hair, turning in circles to search the area, rank frustration displayed on his face.

"It can't be far. It couldn't just disappear, could it?" Emmy replied. She slowly stood up, acutely aware of the rush of bile in the back of her throat. Shaking it off, she clutched her own pack with one fist, unwilling to part with what might be their only bag of supplies.

"I don't know," he said.

They stood in the middle of a wide clearing, encircled by clusters of tall trees. Scattered cat-tail grasses waved in the whisper of cool early evening breeze and the shadow of the setting sun danced along the tree lines. It was impossible to know where they were by the landscape before them, but Emmy was fairly certain the sun set the same way in any time. Soon nightfall would be upon them, so they had little precious time to spare if they wanted to find shelter.

Emmy spotted a break in the clearing. When she squinted her eyes, she could see the irregular outline of something black lying on the ground near the tree line.

"I think I see it," she said, taking off towards it.

"Emmy, wait a second!" Connor objected.

She ignored his suggestion, too intent on recovering his pack. The ground was a bit more loose and deep closer to the trees, turning into a sandy path at the mouth of the woods. With a sign of relief, she picked up Connor's pack, turning towards him with a wide smile.

"See? It's right here. We didn't lose it," she said, thrusting the bag into his hands. He took the bag but his eyes were fixed on something behind her. They were only a few feet into the trees, but she was suddenly aware that she should have waited for him to accompany her. She followed his gaze and turned slowly around, letting her eyes adjust to the dim light inside the dense woods.

Nestled along a wall of flaking slate stone was a small mud and stud cottage built into the rock. One end of the thatched roof was caved in where an overhang sheltered a stack of loose rotted firewood and the wood plank front door hung cock-eyed from one rusted hinge.

"I guess this is where we're meant to be," Connor said.

He brushed past her and approached the house. She watched, wordless, as he tugged on the door and promptly pulled it clear off the hinge, knocking him backward a few steps until he regained his balance. He leaned the door against the frame and stepped inside.

"You can't be serious," she called out. "We're supposed to be in Smithfield in April of 1656. I know I wasn't the best history student, but this doesn't look like anything like a town." He grinned, shrugging his shoulders.

"Well, right now we need a place to stay, 'cause it smells like snow to me," he replied. He wiped his dusty hands off on his jeans and joined her, pointing with one hand at a spot behind her. "Finding shelter is our priority today. We'll figure out exactly where Smithfield is later. And besides, I don't think the owner is going to mind if we hole up here for a bit."

She turned to see what he was pointing at. On the side of the cottage, close to what looked like a small pile of rubble, was a row of headstones. As she approached, she could see words carved into the first stone, but they were crumbling away and difficult to decipher in the fading light so she had to squint.

Thomas Emry
1655

30

It was not an absolute answer to what time they had arrived in, but she assumed it was fairly close. There were two small graves next to him, both of which had a mound of loose fresh soil on top. There were no names on the smaller stones, only a singular cross carved on each, and if she had to guess she would say, by the size, that they were both graves of small children.

"I guess they won't mind," she said softly. Although she did not know them and would likely never know how they died, for a moment she lost herself and mourned the loss of the family that once lived there.

How many events in history were irrevocably linked to other events? Did the family need to die in order for her and Connor to arrive in their time? She could not help wondering if the sequence of events had some greater meaning, some sort of spindly thread tying them all together in some way. The notion that the family of three had to die in order for Connor and Emmy to find shelter when they arrived was just too much to bear, and with that thought, Emmy was reminded of the reason why she had avoided Time Travel for so long.

It was her duty, bound by the ancient blood in her veins and secured on the deathbed of her mother. Emmy promised she would go where the Bloodstone sent her, because mother was certain that Emmy's destiny was linked securely in the past.

"Momma, don't go," Emmy begged, clutching her mother's hand. Mother was frail, and the force of Emmy's fingers made her flinch, causing tears to stream down Emmy's face.

Mother was calm, unmoving on her thick bed of soft white pillows and blankets, her grey eyes steely and certain as she stared at Emmy.

"Promise me," Mother said. Her voice was barely above a whisper, but the stubborn urgency was clear. "Promise me you'll go back. You cannot stay here. You must go where you belong. It's all linked ... and you are part of that link."

When Emmy bowed her head down over her mother's hand and cried, she was not only crying for the loss of her mother. It was the loss of everything she had ever loved, a life in the twenty-first century, the security of being shielded from the horrors of the time her mother was born to, and the desperation of knowing that she was meant to leave the only life she'd ever known. Sobs shook her body, the loss and fear and crushing anguish pouring out at her mother's bedside.

"You cannot run from it, you know," Mother whispered. "May the Gods forgive me, I tried. Don't run, like I did. It's too far gone now to fix, I'm afraid. You must satisfy your place in this world, daughter. We all have a place."

Mother died not long after that, and it was only after they buried her that Connor finally told her the truth. Emmy was listed in the *Leabhar Sinnsreadh*, the Book of the Blooded Ones that mother passed down to him, and Emmy would live her life in the seventeenth century. The first mention of Emmy was in 1656 in Smithfield, Virginia. Connor refused to tell her anything more than that, but it was enough. She'd lived the last few years preparing for it, never truly believing the day would come.

Yet as she stood next to those three lonely graves in the middle of the foreign wilderness, a pang of resolution thudded through her veins and left a burning ache in her chest that threatened to swallow her whole.

"I think you're right," she called out. Her voice was surprisingly steady despite the way she felt shaken to the core of her bones. "This is where we're meant to be. And I think it's the right time."

She shoved her hands into the pockets of her parka and turned to face her brother.

He was right. It did smell like snow, and they needed to find shelter. It was pretty clear that the previous owners would not mind their intrusion. And there was no doubt that they had arrived exactly where they were supposed to be.

THEY LIVED OFF of camping style shrink wrapped meals for a few days while they fortified the abandoned cottage, but Connor started limiting their rations once he had fixed the roof and the door to his satisfaction. It seemed the previous occupants had abruptly moved, leaving an assortment of their belongings behind, and for what they could scavenge from the place they felt fortunate to have. Although they had arrived prepared to travel, it made more sense to prepare the best they could before they set off for Smithfield.

It was no consolation that Conner was right about the weather; on the first night they arrived, a dusting of snow blew in through the damaged roof and blanketed them while they slept, and after a few days of intermittent flurries, a frigid cold front settled in and they were glad they stayed. They spent their time gathering more travel supplies and repairing a lopsided canoe they found in the small barn.

Venturing out away from the cottage became a risky endeavor as the weather worsened, and soon Connor decided he would make one more trade visit with the Ricahecrian tribe settled near the Falls of the James River. They seemed friendly enough and they were more than willing to barter in trade, even for items such as a hunting bow, which Connor acquired on his second trip to the trading post, and a supply of corn, which he acquired as well. A few of them spoke English well enough, and Connor learned that they were near the future city of Richmond, about seventy miles north west of Isle of Wight Shire where they expected to find the small town of Smithfield.

"Well, at least we're only traveling one way," Connor mused one evening as they sat by the fire. He propped one foot up, lounging casually on a thick mat of dried swamp reeds Emmy had found and mended. Unlike Emmy, Connor always dressed in clothes appropriate to the time, wearing brown cotton breeches and a white linen shirt. He dried his tall leather boots by the fire, as they were a bit damp from his latest round of chopping firewood. Running a hand through his thick blond hair, he cocked his head to the side and looked at her.

Emmy nodded in agreement. She closed her hands around her pewter cup, enjoying the warmth that radiated from it due to the sweet hot cherry tea inside.

"Seventy miles on the water is still going to be rough," she added.

"Yeah. Once we get past the falls and the river opens up, it'll be faster. In any case, it's a better alternative than trying to make it by land. Who knows who we'd run into that way. The river's our best bet," Connor replied.

"I know," Emmy said. "I just can't understand for the life of me why we arrived here – and now. It's so damn far from where we need to be. Whoever's in charge of those Bloodstones has a wicked sense of humor."

Connor chuckled. "I guess we'll find out why at some point. There's always a reason, even if it's not plain to us now." He held his cup out for Emmy, and she refilled it from a small pitcher she set next to the fire. He grimaced when he took a long sip, eyeing her with one curiously raised brow.

"Did you add whiskey to this?" he asked, recovering enough to take another swallow.

"A little. I thought we needed it. After all, we're leaving tomorrow after we visit the trading post."

She was surprised to see Connor shake his head.

"I don't want you to go with me this time. I'll go alone and you can wait here," Connor said, changing their intended plan.

"Why? If I don't go with you, it just wastes time," she argued. Emmy had accompanied Connor on several trips to trade with the Ricahecrians.

"Last time I was there – when I went alone – there was an Englishman there named Abraham Wood. He's a slave trader," Connor said. "They're trading slaves, and it looks like it's starting to be a substantial commodity for them. I don't want you anywhere near them after seeing that."

"That's awful," she replied.

"Yeah. I'll get what we need and we'll leave when I return." She nodded and they clinked their cups together in a toast. Connor's eyes drifted to the fire, the strained lines of his face betraying his unease. She let him have his silence without interruption, knowing that the burden of their lives rested on her brother and that it weighed heavily on him.

As the flicker of firelight dimmed, Connor placed another log on the flames and nudged Emmy gently in her side.

"Go to bed. You're dozing off. I'll make sure the fire stays burning," he said. She rubbed her eyes with her closed fists, clutching her blanket around her, and made her way to her cot across the room.

"Emmy?" Connor said some time later, his voice breaking through the recess of her early sleep.

"Hmm?" she replied.

"You know what we agreed on," he said quietly. "If we are parted, you have to carry on. You must get to Smithfield, no matter what happens."

It was a promise easily made at a time she thought she would never need to consider it. When she woke in the morning and Connor was gone, she did not think on it much, but as the day wore on, his words taunted her.

Two days passed and still he did not return. Suddenly everything she knew as right and true seemed like a bleak empty hole in her heart. Yes, she would obey her brother – but he was a bloody fool if he thought she would not try to find him first.

2

The Battle of Bloody Run
James River Falls, 1656
Daniel

THE CURVED EDGE of the gold timepiece was worn smooth against his fingertips, sheltered in the safety of his trouser pocket. Although Daniel wore garments that were a mixture of his native Paspahegh and English style of clothes, he knew the gift for his aunt would stay well protected in the folds of his tunic at his waist. He was confident that when he returned to Basse's Choice, his aunt and uncle would forget the harsh words between them and welcome him home. They would be proud of him for standing in his uncle's place with Colonel Hill. All he needed to do was help the English negotiate an agreement with the Ricahecrians and he would be released from his service. Daniel spent years of his life learning the many languages spoken in Virginia by both the English and the Indian tribes. He was more than ready to be of service and use his skills, despite the order of his uncle to order to leave the English to their own means.

I know what is written in the book, he thought. *It is not yet my time to meet death. My uncle's fears will not sway me from this path.*

As he watched a tall Manahoac brave step away from the other warriors, Daniel dropped his hands to his sides. The man wore his dark hair long and braided, with both sides of his scalp shaved in a crescent shape above his ears. Threaded through his hair was an assortment of dark-tipped feathers and his skin was painted with black and vermilion stain, all evidence of his standing among his peers as a War Chief. His left eye betrayed that he had once been wounded, protruding slightly beneath a ragged patch of scar tissue that extended to his cheek. His attire indicated no influence of the English, being only a simple breechcloth and leggings with a mantle of turkey feathers over his shoulders. Were it another time or another life, Daniel would have liked to know the kinship of such a man, as Daniel only had stories from his uncles to understand what it meant to live the old ways.

Yet today there was no time for such melancholy thoughts. He was allied with the combined Pamunkey and English forces under Colonel Hill as an ambassador, and it was Daniel's job to convince the Ricahecrians that their presence and attempt at a settlement near the falls of the James River should be abandoned. The situation was at a tenuous standstill; on arrival to the village, five Chiefs had approached the Colonial Militia in an attempt to negotiate. Daniel did not know if Colonel Hill gave the order, or if the Militia reacted out of fear, but weapons were drawn and suddenly the Chiefs were captives, surrounded by the English. Now the two sides stood in tense opposition, weapons drawn and tempers flared.

38

Totopotomoi, Weroance to the one hundred Pamunkey warriors aligned with the Colonial Militia, stood with Daniel. His dark eyes betrayed his unease at the situation, and Daniel suspected that Totopotomoi did not agree with Colonel Hill's methods of negotiation. Although Totopotomoi was the half-Pamunkey son of Lord De La Warr, he was a man who held loyalty to his people first, and the English, second. Daniel tilted his head slightly to the side when Totopotomoi spoke to him in his native language.

"I will accompany you to speak with their War Chief. His name is *Wicawa Ni Tu*, Moon Eye to the English, and I am told he is a reasonable man. We must end this now, or I fear the Colonel will provoke an attack," Totopotomoi said, his voice low.

"I agree," Daniel replied, "but I ask that you stay here. They are angered and may choose to take you prisoner, just as we hold their five Chiefs."

"When you go to them alone, they may take you prisoner," Totopotomoi countered.

Daniel nodded. "Yes, perhaps. I am worth nothing to them, as I am only a speaker. Better I be a prisoner, than you. I fear the wrath of my kinswoman if you are away too long from her."

The Weroance grunted a coarse half-laugh. "You know my wife too well. Be on with it, then. Speak boldly, but leave them their pride. One cannot live beside those they conquer if they take their souls from them."

Colonel Hill stiffened at Daniel's right flank and Daniel could feel the weight of the man's stare upon his shoulders, as he was clearly annoyed when the Indians spoke anything other than English. Daniel steadied himself with a deep breath and stood up straight as if a spike was in his spine.

"Is that the one who speaks for them?" Colonel Hill asked, nodding his head in the direction of the War Chief who stood across the clearing.

"I believe so," Daniel replied. "It would show him your good intent if you allow the captured men to stand. You dishonor them by making them kneel. Their War Chief surely considers it an insult."

"The Indians stay where they are for now. Talk to the War Chief and tell him he must take his people and leave. If ye can arrange it, then there will be no bloodshed," the Colonel said.

"Make no move to advance, Colonel. It will serve no one to anger them further," Daniel said. He walked off to meet the War Chief before Colonel Hill could answer. Daniel knew he had no standing to give orders, but if the English truly wanted a peaceable solution, then they needed to hear his counsel.

As he met with the War Chief in the middle of the clearing, he tried to forget about the five Ricahecrian Chiefs on their knees behind him, held at gunpoint by the Colonial Militia. Although he was Paspahegh, and by the lineage of his blood, loyal to what remained of the Powhatan, the thought of those proud warriors kneeling on the frozen earth shamed him. They were his people, just as the English were his people by virtue of his mother's English blood that graced his veins. Yet in that moment, Daniel was utterly alone. It was the truth that plagued him his entire life; he did not truly belong to either side. He had no loyalty, other than to what he must do. It was his duty to make the Ricahecrians see reason, to convince them to leave the Falls.

"I am Daniel Neilsson, and I speak for Colonel Hill of the Colonial Militia of Virginia, and Totopotomoi, Weroance of the Pamunkey," Daniel offered. The War Chief's lips curled back into a sneer.

"I know who you are. I know why you are here. I am Wicawa Ni Tu. Release our men and then we will talk," the warrior replied.

Daniel wished he had the power to grant that request, for he knew that the gesture would resonate with the Ricahecrian. Daniel felt the hollow echo of regret as he stared at the man in front of him. Were they not both from the same lands, made from the Great Creator and blessed with the blood of the earth in their veins? No, Wicawa Ni Tu was not an ally, but instead an enemy, and by his unauthorized settlement close to English lands, Wicawa Ni Tu and his people were now enemies of the Governor of Virginia. With all of the strength in his heart, Daniel prayed the warrior would agree to leave peacefully; Daniel wished no more bloodshed of any First People on the soil of what was once the Great Lands of Tsenacommacah.

"It is not my order to give. Colonel Hill will release them when you agree to return to your own lands. The English claim this land, and they do not give you permission to stay."

Wicawa Ni Tu scowled at Daniel's declaration and his hand slipped down to his side to rest over the butt of the knife at his belt. Daniel did not waver, continuing to keep his eyes level with the man. For a long moment they stared at each other, until Wicawa Ni Tu broke the silence with a wry grin and shake of his head, the grey and black feathers tied in his hair bobbing with the motion.

"Daniel *Neilsson*," the warrior said. "I know of your uncle, *Winkeohkwet*. Like you, he too has aligned with the English. Perhaps your sense has been twisted by him, just as he was twisted by his ties to the Time Walkers."

Daniel kept his face passive in a show of disinterest, but the mention of his family's secret sent a spike of panic through his chest. *What exactly did Wicawa Ni Tu know about his family, and what was his purpose in speaking of them?*

"My uncle calls for peace, as do I," he replied, his voice low.

Wicawa Ni Tu's eyes narrowed. "So say you," he replied. "Tell me, then, Daniel Neilsson. What will you give me for this trade? What I require from you is a simple thing."

"And what, may I ask, do you require of me?" Daniel returned.

"Many of our people are sick. They are plagued by a fever and suffer in pain for weeks, and many more die than live. I need the blood of a Time Walker to cure them."

"I am filled with sorrow for your people, but Time Walkers no longer live among us. Opechancanough ensured their deaths many years ago," Daniel said. Wicawa Ni Tu was persistent, however, and Daniel could see the agitation rise in the creased features of his face beneath the paint stains on his skin.

"If that is so, then why do I hold one here as my prisoner?" Wicawa Ni Tu demanded. He raised his hand and barked a command in his own tongue, and two warriors dragged a man forward. It was a white man, dressed in the torn brown wool breeches of an

42

Englishman, with a flash of ragged blond hair and his head hanging limp as if he were unconscious. There were bandages on both of his wrists, and dark bruises littering his pale flesh. When the men released him, he collapsed to the ground, reaching out with shaking hands in an attempt to lift himself from the cold earth.

Wicawa Ni Tu snatched one of the captive's hands, wrenching it outward from the groaning man to ensure Daniel could see the scar upon the man's palm. Daniel froze.

He knew the mark. It was the mark of a Bloodstone, borne by those who traveled through time – the same mark that graced the hand of the Time Walkers he called kin.

"I have bled him, but he is weak. He is not strong enough to heal my people. I need another, one with more powerful blood. I hear tales that the women are most powerful, so bring me one of those. This one has a woman hidden somewhere, maybe he has children; he trades supplies with us and my men have seen her with him. Bring me a woman Time Walker and I will sign your treaty. I will lead my people away from these lands."

The captive raised his head, enough so that Daniel could catch a glimpse of his battered face. He was a young man of about Daniel's age, perhaps older. He was not of Daniel's kin, and for that he was grateful, but he was a Time Walker, and Daniel felt some duty towards him. *Where did he come from? Who were his people?*

"I do not know this man, nor his kin. I cannot give you what I do not have," Daniel said slowly, shifting his eyes away from the captive. Seeing the Time Walker unsettled him, but he could not allow it to sway him. It was clear that Wicawa Ni Tu heard the legends and knew the healing powers Time Walkers possessed, yet the Ricahecrian did not know how to wield the power that he sought to control. The very notion of one man using the sacred blood to fulfill his own needs was the same reason that the Blooded Ones stayed in hiding.

Wicawa Ni Tu dropped the captive's hand. He stalked over to Daniel, stopping only a pace away. Daniel held his ground, refusing to show the man any sign of weakness.

"I want the rest of his kind. Do not speak untruth to me. I know you know where they hide, just as your uncle protected them from Opechancanough's wrath. Bring them to me and we will settle this now."

Daniel thought of the men behind him. Daniel was not in command, he was only the voice between the factions. It was Colonel Hill who decided their fate, and Totopotomoi who led the Pamunkey warriors who stood with the English. Daniel felt the spirits of his ancestors as he walked alone, for it was only them that could comfort him when he was the spawn of two worlds which might never be at peace.

What choice did he have? The life of a stranger he might never find, in lieu of peace? In that moment, it was an easy request to grant. Although a part of him screamed that he had no right to barter such a thing, he had no other means to end it.

"I will try to find his kind," Daniel said. The words felt like sand in his throat. "If I succeed, I will bring them to you. You have my word on this. And now I ask for your word in return."

Wicawa Ni Tu nodded. "So it is. Tell your English Colonel we will leave. We will seek other lands west of here. And when you find the family of my Time Walker," he said, his voice low and purposeful, "You will bring them to me."

It was done.

Yet it was not finished. As Daniel moved to clasp the warrior's arm, the scream of gunfire pierced the silence and he could smell the thick scent of gunpowder infuse the air. He swung swiftly around to the sound in time to see the first Chief face down on the ground, hands bound behind his back, and then another shot echoed and the wails of helpless denial streamed forth from the Ricahecrian people as the second Chief was shot. The Militia picked off the rest in short order, leaving the five bodies on the frozen ground as warriors scattered around them. Bellowed war cries filled the space and the bodies of men in battle crashed together around him.

Raw instinct took over. Daniel reached for his knife and faced Wicawa Ni Tu, but the War Chief was surrounded by a thick throng of armed men and Daniel could only see his face through the crowd. Someone shoved him, and then he was grabbed by the arm. It was Totopotomoi, his eyes filled with fire.

"Take this!" the Weroance shouted, shoving a long-handled ax into Daniel's hand. Around them, the Pamunkey clashed with the Ricahecrians, and Daniel immediately noticed that there were very few of their Colonial Militia allies fighting beside them.

Had he ever truly expected it to come to bloodshed? Daniel had never been in battle, and at that moment standing beside Totopotomoi, the reality of it came crashing down. When he looked at the mythical Pamunkey Chief standing beside him, flinging off attacks with the blows of his club despite the surge of warriors that descended upon them, Daniel knew why his uncle ordered him to leave the English to their own battles.

"Fall back!" Colonel Hill commanded in English. *"Fall back!"* Most of the Pamunkey could not understand the call, nor did they have any means to retreat since they were the barrier between the Ricahecrians and the English. *The English were leaving.* The Militia obeyed the orders immediately, as if they expected the command to come, and it was only moments before the Pamunkey warriors were left to face the massive Ricahecrian forces alone.

"By the Creator," Totopotomoi muttered, swinging his club low to take an attacker out at the knees. The motion flipped the man onto his back before the Weroance made the killing blow by smashing the club to his head with a spray of gore. The copper bracelets on the Chief's lean arms reflected the setting sun and his body seemed swallowed in an ethereal glow, his long, feather adorned braid swinging like a banner streaming out behind him as he whirled and faced his enemies.

Daniel backed up to Totopotomoi and brandished his own weapon. Daniel could hear the whisper of his uncle Winn's last words to him, a bitter premonition of warning that inflamed the panic roaring between his ears.

"Why will you not stand beside them? Is it not your duty to save our kind from more bloodshed with the English?" Daniel demanded of his uncle. Winn watched Colonel Hill and his Militia ride away from their farm on the outskirts of Basse's Choice.

Winn uttered a coarse grunt, more of a half-laugh, as if the very notion of Daniel questioning his decisions was an amusing matter.

"Yes, I serve as a speaker for them, as I once did for Opechancanough when he asked it of me. Time has passed and the path is a different one now. My duty is here, standing beside me," Winn said, placing a hand on Daniel's shoulder as he met his gaze, "and it is there, inside that house. That is the only duty I know above all else, and it is for all of you that I will not sway from it." Winn glanced towards the house where Daniel's aunt and cousins were still sleeping. The gesture was not lost on Daniel, but still, the stubbornness in his soul still surged.

"You have that duty, uncle. Not I. I am only the half-English son of a dead Paspahegh warrior. What duty do I have here, or anywhere else? I have none but what I will make in the time left to me in this life. If I help them, then perhaps I will be a part of something that matters. Perhaps I will be remembered when I am gone," Daniel replied. "I know when my spirit will leave this earth, and it will not be when I stand beside Colonel Hill. I still have time."

Winn sighed. His fingers dug into Daniel's shoulder, his dark eyes reflecting his sadness. Daniel did not like knowing he hurt his uncle, nor did he wish to cause him any worry. Yet if anyone in his life could understand what it was like to know your fate before it happened, then it was Winn, and Daniel did not fear seeking his own path to that place.

"It will not be what you want of it, nephew," Winn said quietly. "When you offer yourself to them, it may be a debt you can never repay."

"I hear you, uncle."

Yet Daniel regretted those words. As he struck the next man who approached and then moved with Totopotomoi to a place of slight cover near a grove of dense trees, Daniel wondered if he would have any chance to mend things with his family – or if he might ever see them again.

Shrieks from the dying came from the battlefield. A blow came to his head from behind, glancing off his ear but leaving a warm gush of blood dripping down his face. Daniel ducked as the Ricahecrian swung again, this time making contact with the side of his ax into the man's flank. The blow was not without consequence, leaving Daniel's head swimming and his vision dangerously clouded while he struggled to regain his footing. He stumbled to the side, away from the fallen man.

A few feet away stood Totopotomoi, surrounded by three Ricahecrian men. For the rest of his days when Daniel recalled that moment, what would follow him most was the way the Chief's eyes betrayed his fierce resolve.

Totopotomoi knew it was his time – his gaze was raw and wild and clear – but it was evident he would take many with him when he fell. Bracing himself in a crouch with the spread of his eagle feather mantle flaring wide across his back, the world exploded around him and he started to move. It was a torturous slow dance, the song of a soul and the whisper of defiance, and it played before Daniel's eyes as if the remnants of some legendary tale. His mantle swirled around him with each strike; Totopotomoi felled two men before the blow came that sent him to his knees.

Daniel shouted his name, his eyes blurred and unseeing from blood or tears he did not know, and it was as the wind left his lungs that he felt the stab to the flesh at his side. It was quick and precise, a strike from the knife of the man at his feet that Daniel thought he had killed.

He fell to the ground, dropping his ax, one hand outstretched to land in the cold mud. Although the fingers of his other hand sought to clutch the wound at his side, when he pulled back his hand he could see it was covered in his own blood.

Had he known what was to come, would he still have traveled that same path? Not only for knowing that it *would* end, as all lives do, but for the when and how of it?

3

Emmy

HER LEGS ACHED and her tired muscles screamed in protest with each step she took. The handgun tucked between her jeans and underwear on her lower back was rubbing her raw after hours of walking, so she repositioned it and placed it on her right side. She was vaguely aware of the pang of hunger in her belly and the way her lips were cracked and dry, but her satchel was empty and her canteen had only a few drops of water left. According to the position of the setting sun above her head, it was well past the time that she should have returned to the cottage.

It was yet another day that Connor failed to return home. At first she was sure he'd be back with much needed food, giving her some ridiculous excuse for why he had been gone so long. As the days stretched into a week, however, her faith was beginning to falter and a rising sting of hopelessness pricked at her every thought.

What if something had happened to him? What if he never returned?

She clenched her fist and wiped a tear angrily from the edge of her eye. She knew he would never stay away this long if it was within his control. Connor was the confident one, the strong one between them. He was unrelenting in his faith that they were meant to be in the seventeenth century and that they would make it to Smithfield before winter was fully upon them. It should have been one last exchange at the trading post gathering travel supplies and trading with the Ricahecrians in preparation for their journey. There was nothing that would sway him from returning to her – unless something had gone terribly wrong.

A familiar patch of trees up ahead gave her some measure of relief. On a low hanging branch, she spotted a flash of bright red flannel, a piece of her spare shirt that stood out against the greens and browns of the woods and served as her own personal breadcrumb trail. Since she realized she was relatively close to the cottage, she took her flask and tilted the rim to her lips, swallowing the last of her walking supply. There was a stream nearby and she could fill it back up before she returned to the house to do the same thing she had done every night since Connor had left – eat enough to sustain herself, decide on a search plan for the next day, and pray that Connor was not dead in a ditch somewhere, or worse. As much as she wished to deny it, her only option left was to travel to the Ricahecrian village and inquire if Connor ever made it there.

She pushed through the dense weeds and kneeled down at the edge of the creek, thrusting her canteen beneath the water. It was a source she knew to be clean, as neither she nor Connor had suffered any ill effects after drinking from it, and since she was alone she was not willing to risk trying anything new. Although she had been schooled in rudimentary survival and she was knowledgeable of the mid-seventeenth century tidewater region, she did not feel safe enough to roam too far from her shelter. Reality was harsh; the natives were not always friendly and the English were no better. A single woman dressed in men's clothes traipsing through the woods alone was a recipe for disaster no matter who she might run into.

As she screwed the cap on the canteen and stood up, a flock of birds left their nests in a rush of feathers and squalls as if a predator disturbed them, and when she looked back down, she thought she noticed an odd color to the creek water. A rush of nausea hit her at the same time, setting her head to spinning despite her attempt to steady herself. *No time for déjà vu* she thought, shaking her head. Thinking her eyes were just tired, she blinked and stuck her fingers into the current, letting the water wash over her hand.

Red.

The water was tinged red.

She heard him moan before she spotted him lying on the creek bank. Her heart pounded madly in her ears when she realized there was a trail of blood where the man had crawled from the water, pooling from a wound on his side that soaked through his tunic. It was not Connor, for which she was grateful, but as she walked closer she could see the man had dark hair tied in a knot with a braid of rawhide twisted at his nape. He was tall, even taller than her brother, and in taking a closer look at him, she noted he wore copper beads strung through a string around his neck.

A native. Was he dead?

The last of the sunset was dipping down behind her, casting the man in the shadow of her body when she stood next to him. She could almost hear her brother's

52

voice hollering at her to turn and run, but in the absence of any good sense, she was frozen in place.

Should she help him? What if more of them came looking for him? She had two bullets left in her gun, and if Connor did not return soon she was acutely aware it was her only means of defending herself.

She was considering her options when he reached out and latched onto her ankle. His clammy hand settled in a surprisingly firm grip directly above her leather work boot, smearing her with his blood yet still holding her tightly.

"Take me home," he said, his English heavily accented but clear. "I am ready now."

His motion was enough to snap her back to reality. She did not have the luxury of time nor resources to deal with a dying man, and she especially did not intend to be a victim if he was suddenly making a miraculous recovery. Alone, afraid, and utterly at the end of her rope, she leaned down and looked at his face. He looked harmless enough, but she couldn't afford to take any chances.

She pulled the gun from her jeans.

"Christ!" she muttered. She couldn't shoot him; as much as she'd been trained to leave emotions behind and do what needed to be done, she couldn't make herself pull that trigger on a living human being. And besides, she only had two bullets left, and he looked halfway dead to begin with. Connor might think her a coward, but so be it.

His grip tightened and she panicked. She made her decision, letting loose a rash of furious curse words that would have made a sailor blush.

"Not today," she insisted, talking more to herself than to him. "Not today. I am *not* doing this bullshit today!"

She slammed the butt of the gun down on his temple, releasing his hold and knocking him flat on the ground. Bending at the knee, she parted his bloody tunic and quickly examined the wound. It wasn't anything like Connor's gunshot wound. This was clean and exact, more likely to have come from a knife or some other sort of sharp weapon. He might live, if he was tended to.

"Damn it," she whispered.

Well, better get moving, she thought. If she couldn't kill him, she certainly couldn't leave him there to suffer. She didn't have any more vials of her newborn blood, but she had some supplies and a pretty decent background in emergency care. Connor was the doctor in the family, and as she looped the nylon strap of her canteen under the man's arms and started dragging him with it, she vaguely recalled something about the Hippocratic Oath, *"do no harm"*, and wondered if it applied to her by default.

4

Daniel

HE WOKE TO the sensation of heat on his skin, washing over him like the gentle whisper of a mother's touch to wake him from his slumber. Losing himself in the beauty of that caress was easy; pushing it aside to reach the barrier of consciousness, however, was another matter.

A whiff of charred pine boughs seemed grossly out of place for what he imagined the afterlife would be. Daniel cracked his eyelids open into slits, only enough to see his surroundings, allowing a glimpse of amber firelight that made him wince. At once, he spotted his clothes set out on a stone hearth by the fire, and he could see a bundle of his belongings tied neatly together with his knife laying on top.

He was not too concerned with the stab of pain that tore through his belly when he moved, because he was too focused on his hands being tied to the bedding platform. Jerking his wrist, he tried to shake it off, yet both his hands were bound with thick rope and would not budge.

"Won't do you any good."

A woman stood in front of him, hands crossed over the swell of her breasts as she leveled a confident stare at him. *Was she the one who had knocked him out?* His head felt like a jumbled mess of chaos stuffed between his ears, so he wasn't sure of anything at that moment.

"Stop thrashing," she said, approaching the bed. He did not recognize her curious accent, nor did she look like any English lady he had ever known. She peered down at him and suddenly scowled, her wide lips pursed and her eyes narrowed. "You'll open your stitches. Are you *trying* to bleed to death?" she demanded.

He did not move when she sat down beside him on the bed. She worked swiftly, peeling the bandage on his left lower belly slightly back so that she could look inside. She dabbed at the wound with a piece of white cloth and uttered a sort, tight-lipped sigh.

"Am I bleeding to death?" he asked quietly. His throat burned with thirst and it was difficult to croak out the words through his parched lips, yet he was genuinely interested in her opinion of his situation. It was clear she was no angel sent to guide him to the afterlife, and since he was firmly still planted on the earth, he resorted to trying to befriend his captor. The sooner he gained her trust and convinced her to remove his bindings, the sooner he could empty his bladder. In the state he was currently confined to, however, he feared that if she pressed on his abdomen any more, the decision would be taken from both of their control.

"Well, not right now. But if you keep that up, you will," she replied, tucking the bandage back into place. As she bent her head to the task, her long honey-streaked hair tickled his chest. She brushed her hair absently behind her ear with one hand, surveying her work with a nod. Her fingers slid over the skin near his navel, sending a rush of heat straight down to his toes

56

which caused him to recoil and try to sink down into the mattress.

"Untie me," he ground out through gritted teeth. She glanced up, her expression changing from satisfied to suspicious in the span of a moment.

"I'm sure you understand why I can't do that. I'm sorry, I don't know who you are, or anything about you," she said. "I have to protect myself until we come to an agreement."

He swallowed hard. "I have no intention of harming you, and I would like to extend my thanks for your kind care. But you need to untie me *right now*."

She stood up and stepped back. Although her presence sent his senses reeling and each touch of her hand reminded him more of his bodily functions, seeing her move away was even worse.

"You'll stay tied for now," she said.

"For the love of the Gods, woman, give me at least one of my hands and the use of that pewter pot," Daniel replied evenly, "Unless you wish to assist me in an even more personal manner than tending my wound."

Her jaw dropped and her mouth formed a small circle, her cheeks bursting with a rash of crimson as she appeared to have gleaned his meaning. Daniel wasn't in the habit of speaking so coarsely in the presence of the fair gender, but for all his manners and attempts at niceties, the damnable woman needed a direct explanation to understand his need. Could she not *see* that the only thing on his mind was relieving his water?

She moved quickly. The knots came free with a few tugs, and he was surprised after all of her staunch bluster that she untied both of his hands. He rolled onto his side as soon as he was free, clenching the edge of the bed as a wave of nausea hit him and a cold sweat broke out across his forehead. Trying to stay out of her way and clutching the bedding to his waist so as not to alarm her, he attempted to sit up, yet she slipped her hands around his upper arm and pulled his weight onto her in support.

"Here, lean on me if you're standing up, or I'm afraid you'll fall," she advised him. The bedding was askew and he resigned to letting it fall to the floor, leaving himself exposed but having no alternative since his clothes were across the room. He lifted an eyebrow and glanced sideways at her, taking the pewter pot that she offered him. The throbbing pain in his side was reduced for the moment, muted by the situation he found himself in.

"Thank ye," he said softly. "I should not like to fall after all your efforts to bring me to good health. Yet it is not proper for you to help me further, so be assured, I will abide fine if you step away."

Her lips thinned and turned up in the hint of a smile.

"I've been taking care of you for three days, and it's not the first time you've had to do that," she replied. She let out a muffled laugh and turned her back to him when the sound of his stream pinged in the pewter pot. The relief was immediate, and after the initial rush he noticed her hands were crossed over her chest again and that she was tapping her foot on the plank floor.

"Then I must beg your pardon, miss, for what you have endured."

"It wasn't that bad," she said.

The strength faded from his limbs seemingly with the draining of his bladder. He finally finished and placed the pot on a chair next to the bed, taking the breeches that she thrust at him with her back still turned.

"Do you need help?"

"No," he insisted. He managed to slide into the breeches and sit back down on the edge of the bed, his vision swirling dangerously while he was bathed in clammy sweat from the pain in his side.

Although he had enough good sense to know he was injured, his stubborn pride was still foremost in his mind. It unnerved him to be weak under her watchful eye, nothing more than an ailing stranger to the slip of a woman staring him down. He watched her fumble for something by the hearth, noting the way her loose long hair nearly touched the belt of her strange blue trousers. The color of her hair was unlike any he had ever seen on any English woman or native, a light russet brown shade with honey-colored streaks scattered throughout. Even dressed in a man's clothes, she would never be mistaken for anything but a female.

"Go ahead and lay back down. I'll leave you untied for now," she said, turning around. She leveled what looked like a rather small flintlock pistol at him, holding it surprisingly steady in her hands. For a moment he considered trying to reason with her, but he dismissed that thought and resigned himself to obeying her commands. Perhaps if she gained some measure of comfort, she would see he meant her no harm.

"Of course," he replied. He wanted to remain upright so that he might speak with her, yet the wound in his side was more tolerable when he laid flat. She seemed placated by his acquiescence and he wondered what horrors had befallen her that she was so afraid of one wounded man.

As far as he could see, her belongings were sparse. There was some sort of satchel on the floor near the hearth. Along the corner of the room was another small cot, sectioned off with a blanket strung up with brown twine tied to the rafters. He spotted a dark blue dress that resembled what an English lady might wear, with a long white linen shift hanging by a hook on the wall. When he returned his gaze to the woman, her wide green eyes met his.

"You speak English," she said. It was forced from her lips as an accusation, one he must account for.

"I do," he said slowly, keeping his eyes locked with hers. "I was raised in a place where English words are spoken, among others."

"What village are you from? Will they come looking for you?" she asked. She gradually lowered the gun but kept her distance, choosing to sit down on a stool near the second cot in the corner.

"I live at Basse's Choice. They will not look for me. I'm sure they believe I am dead," he replied. The truth of his situation felt heavy in his chest, yet if sharing the knowledge with her would ease her fears, then he would tell her whatever she wished to know. Suddenly, looking into her wary eyes, he wanted nothing more than to give her comfort. "My name is Daniel Neilsson."

"Are you Nansemond? I thought Nansemonds lived at Basse's Choice by now? I've never heard of an Indian named Neilsson," she said. It was more of a statement than anything, her eyebrows scrunched up as if she were mulling it over in her head.

"My father was Paspahegh. I live with my uncle's family, brother to my father. My uncle was born of a Norseman and his Paspahegh wife, and as such, he calls his family *Neilsson*. 'Tis a long story, and one I am glad to share with you, if you had some time to spare."

She broke into a smile. "Oh, I think I have a few minutes."

It was a welcome distraction from their predicament and Daniel joined her with a grin of his own. He leaned up on one elbow, taking care not to stretch his wound too much yet giving him a better view of her. The urge to know her suddenly drove him to distraction, and he had the unsettling notion that it would take him the rest of his years to ever be satiated of looking upon her.

"And you? Where do you hail from, and who are your people?" he asked.

Her throat contracted and her cheeks flushed once more.

"I'm Emmy. Emmy Cameron. My brother and I live here – he'll be back anytime. He's just hunting," she said hurriedly.

He did not miss the inflection in her words, or the abrupt way her jovial mood dimmed. In all of his days, he had never seen a woman behave so plainly, with every bit of her emotion on display like a brave banner flaming in the sun. In the span of a quarter hour, she had run the gauntlet of fear, conquered it with fiery resolve, then exposed her sorrow in a moment of weakness. He knew then that she was either lying about having a brother, or more likely, something had happened to her brother. It was enough to explain the mercurial mood and her underlying fear among her dismal living quarters.

"You must be hungry. I – I can get you a bowl of stew, if you feel up to it, that is. I mean, you've only taken in a bit of broth for the past three days," she said carefully.

She cloaked her emotions well, closing down to further questions with a shrug. In that moment, he wanted to forget all that had brought him there, or that he needed to return to the Pamunkey village and bring news of the battle deaths. He wanted to ignore the questions he should be asking, and lose himself in the complexity of the woman before him. Before him was a woman who had given of herself to a stranger, putting aside her own troubles to unselfishly save his life. He could see the toll it took on her by the way her hands shook when she sat down beside him with the bowl of stew, and by the way her eyes darted nervously every few minutes back to the gun she left on the table.

They made pleasant small talk after that while he ate. The stew tasted good, but he noticed there was only a small bit of lean rabbit meat in it along with a hard crust of bread. How long had she made the meat of a rabbit last? And what would she do when it ran out?

He kept his worries to himself, choosing to keep their banter light. When darkness swallowed the tiny cottage and the fire was banked and low, she stood up in the glow of the dying embers and looked out the lone glass pane window. The telltale kiss of winter had arrived. Snow was falling, and for all he was as a man he would have done anything to prevent the look of desolation on her face when she saw it. She glanced slightly backward at him, the outline of her face tilted, and he was helpless to comfort her when the reality of their situation hit them both.

"I don't know when Connor will be home," she said softly, her voice trailing off as if she regretted saying it aloud.

He knew as well as she did that travel in the snow was dangerous. They were trapped together in that cottage, one injured man and one woman full of secrets. The gravity of it felt heavy in his chest. After all she had done for him, there was nothing else he could do for her except give her a few hours of peace.

"We shall speak more tomorrow, Miss Cameron," he said. He held his hands out to her, so that when she raised her eyes to look at him, she was presented with his upturned palms. "Bind me and take your rest. I'll be no worry to you while you sleep, and in the morning, perhaps this storm will pass."

It was all he could give her, and by the way her shoulders slumped and the breath left her body in a long sigh, he knew he had helped to ease her mind a bit. He patiently held his wrists at his sides while she bound them to the bed, closing his eyes briefly when she leaned over him and her hair brushed his cheek.

"Miss Cameron," he asked, daring one last question before he left her to her slumber. "How did you bring me here?"

The edge of her plump lip twisted in a smile.

"Why, I dragged you, of course," she replied.

He nodded. *She was stronger than she looked.* A grown man would have a difficult time of dragging Daniel's solid body a few feet, yet somehow she had managed it without help. *Pity the man who looks upon this mite of a woman and thinks he might best her,* he thought with a smile.

She went about her business in the corner of the cottage, drawing the makeshift drape closed. It was curious that she left a candle burning and he wondered why she might waste it for the task of sleeping, yet the distraction of watching her shadow behind the drape quickly drove the question from his mind. He could see the outline of her body in the flicker of the dim candle light as she undressed but it made him feel ashamed to look at her in such a way, so he turned his head away from her and was content to merely listen to the sounds of her slumber for the rest of the night.

5

Emmy

THERE WAS A sleeping, half-naked wounded man who might very well kill her tied to a bed across the room, and all she could focus on was what she should wear. It wasn't a completely idiotic thought, despite the outward appearance of such a frivolous notion, but more of a desperate way of getting control of a situation that was rapidly spinning out of her hands. She had already said too much to the man, revealing that Connor was gone. Smacking her flattened palm against her forehead, she let out a long sigh.

She needed to be careful. Yes, she had saved his life, but she was under no illusion that he might harbor any sense of loyalty to her. After all, as far as he knew, she was just an English woman living on a secluded homestead. Despite his claim that he lived on the outskirts of Jamestown at Basse's Choice, and that he came from some sort of mixed community, the threat was still very real.

A Paspahegh? Emmy knew her history well – hell, it had been a subject hammered into her head since she was old enough to read! She was certain that the

Paspahegh people had been one of the first to encounter the English at the Jamestown settlement in 1607, however all trace of the Paspahegh people was gone from the written record by 1611. The Paspahegh were known by history to have both succumbed to diseases brought by the settlers and then eradicated in skirmishes with the English. So when Daniel claimed to be the son of a Paspahegh brave, it threw her for a loop, as did his notion that his uncle was half *Norse*.

"Yeah, right. He's out of his mind," Emmy snorted. She didn't intend for her thought to be verbal, but it slipped out nonetheless. The notion that there were any Norseman settled in the region was just too far-fetched to even consider. She simply could not believe that her knowledge of history was that off-base.

With the snow still falling heavily and no signs of it stopping that morning, harsh reality was that they were stuck together until it let up. She needed to quell any suspicions he might have over her strange attire, and then she needed to gain his trust.

The blue dress, she thought, glancing at the garment. She did not like wearing the thing, and although she was quite aware that she needed to dress the part of the time, she still regressed to wearing her own comfortable clothes when she was hunting. Connor would flip his lid if he knew she wore her jeans and a heavy parka while she was searching for him, and it would be difficult to explain herself should she meet anyone along the way. She could hear the echo of his words rush through her thoughts. *"We need to acclimate," Connor said, shortly after they arrived. "This is our home now. We have to fit in."*

Connor was right, as always. And if wearing a damn ridiculous dress made her fit in with the time, then she had to do it. Later she could try to figure out how women actually *functioned* with layers of skirts impeding their every move, and exactly how they managed to pee without soaking themselves, but for now she'd just deal with it.

She resigned herself to dressing, pulling the white cotton chemise over her head. The stiff whalebone stays remained sitting on the stool; there was no way she was asking Daniel to help her with it, and she was not able to fasten it herself. She managed to adjust the dress overtop of the chemise with little trouble, smoothing down the split layered skirt so that the petticoat was in the proper place. It fit snugly enough considering it was just a reproduction costume she'd failed to return from an upscale costume rental place in Philadelphia.

Daniel was awake when she pushed the curtain back, his dark eyes meeting hers the moment she came into view. She felt an immediate surge of heat rush to her cheeks at the connection, embarrassed and awkward in the ungainly dress and utterly bothered that she appeared like such a nervous idiot in front of him. She was stronger than that, and she closed her hands into fists and dug her nails into her palms as she silently berated herself.

He was just a man, after all, and she had her gun to protect herself.

"I – I need to put some corn cobs out, and then I'll unite you," she announced. She meant to assure him that she was in charge of the situation, reminding herself that she was perfectly capable of dealing with him.

"Might you untie me first? Unless you wish to be here again when I use the pot?" he replied, his voice betraying his jovial mood. She scowled and stalked over to him, hastily untying his bonds.

No, she certainly did *not* want to see him half-clothed again.

He sat up on the edge of the bed. The curve of his lips twitched as if he found her amusing, and she thought she heard him chuckle when she grabbed the bag of corn cobs from the hearth and slammed the door.

She hadn't bothered to put on her cloak and she immediately regretted it. Although the snowfall had slowed somewhat, it was still wet and cold, and trudging through it in her laced leather boots only led to her bare legs turning to ice. She tossed corncobs and food scraps around the edge of the clearing and emptied the bag quickly, past caring at that point if it mattered or not. With all the snow on the ground she wasn't going to risk being outside hunting for very long, and she was pretty sure any of the wildlife she was trying to attract wasn't going to walk around in it either.

When she went back inside, Daniel was sitting on a stool next to the fire, pushing a new log up onto the flame with a long stick. He wore only his breeches and she could see a dark stain of blood soaked partially through the bandage around his waist.

"It doesn't look like it's stopping anytime soon," she commented. Perhaps if they talked about something like the weather, it would distract her from the pressing fears in her mind. Namely, that Connor was hurt or trapped somewhere, and that she could no longer search for him until the weather broke.

68

Or the nagging truth that she had to go to the trading post to look for him alone, and if that was not successful, she would have to find her own way to Smithfield to satisfy the vow they had taken.

"Perhaps another day or two," Daniel replied. "When the storm breaks, I will take my leave. I thank ye for your kind care."

She eyed him warily. Yes, he was sitting up and had managed to get across the room without her assistance, but the wound on his side was not yet healed.

"You're welcome," she said. She busied herself by shaking the snow from her boots and taking them off, careful to put them far enough away from the fire that they would not get burned, but close enough to dry in the heat of the flame. "How far away is Basse's Choice? You said that's where you live, right?"

"Yes, that is my home. But I will not return there."

"Where will you go?" she asked.

The side of his jaw tightened as took a sip from a pewter cup and swallowed. "I need to bring word to the wife of my *Weroance*. She should hear what fate has befallen her husband, and as she is my kin, it should come from my lips."

His words made sense. She suspected he was not alone and that he was involved in some sort of skirmish.

"Was it – was it an attack? Is that how you were wounded?" she asked. He quieted, looking down at the cup in his hands for a moment before he met her gaze. She immediately regretted prying when she noted the sadness in his gaze. It lingered there between them, frozen like the hardened ground, until he spoke again.

69

"It should not have happened. I stood beside an Englishman and asked the Pamunkey to trust him," Daniel said quietly, his voice no more than a hum over the sound of the crackling fire. "Yet I was wrong. We were betrayed, and now all the Pamunkey warriors are dead. Even my cousin's husband, Totopotomoi – a great *Weroance*. I do not know how I will tell my cousin he is dead, but I must."

Emmy did not know what to say. She wanted to comfort him somehow, but the idea that she might have the power to ease his trouble seemed beyond any skill she possessed. She could tend his wound and urge him towards physical recovery, but the damage to his haunted soul was another matter. The truth was that as much as she had prepared to travel to the past, nothing could have prepared her for the reality of living it. Yes, she had read about the long history of battles between the Indians and the settlers, but hearing it come from the mouth of the man sitting beside her was beyond the scope of her imagination.

"I'm so sorry," she whispered. *At least he doesn't know what will happen to his people*, she thought. *At least he doesn't know that horrible truth.*

He nodded without answering her. His lips twisted a bit and his brows knotted downward, the whites of his knuckles standing out as he gripped the pewter cup. At a loss to say anything sensible, she decided to tend to something she could fix, and that was his bandage. She dropped down on one knee beside him and reached for the knot.

"I think the bleeding is stopped for the most part," she said. She peered inside the loosened wrap, content to see the stitches intact. The blood was dark and dried, and likely from him tossing in his sleep during the night.

"Thank you," he said.

"You're welcome."

As she stood up, he caught the tips of her fingers in his hand. His touch was firm yet gentle, his motions reflecting the deep discord behind his sorrowful eyes.

"I would like to repay you for your kindness. Do you have any weapons here?" he asked. She should have felt uneasy at his question but she did not, too focused on the warmth of his touch as he held her hand.

"Other than my gun?" she replied. "I have a few knives. Oh, and there's a bow that my brother left. I only have two bullets left for the gun, so I can't use that." He stood up, lessening the space between them. "Why do you ask?"

"I see your stores run low. I can hunt for you before I leave. The bow will suffice."

Hunt for her? How on earth was he going to do that, when only less than a week ago he'd nearly bled to death from his wounds? She couldn't say the offer was not attractive – hell, she had used the rest of her dried rabbit meat the day he woke up. Yet it was the intent of his request that stirred her, and suddenly she realized how bone-tired she was from just simply trying to *survive.*

"I would appreciate that, but you're not ready to hunt. The snow's at least a foot deep, and I haven't seen any game for a week," she countered.

"Would you have me at your mercy longer than necessary?" he replied with a grin edging his lips. She snorted a muffled laugh.

71

"You're not much trouble." Her instincts should be screaming at her to gladly see him on his way, since she had no assurance of his true intention. Despite her better judgment and his close proximity, she smiled. She squinted when their eyes met and a flush of heat spiked her skin, causing him to grin.

"Well, trouble or not, I am in your debt, Miss Cameron. Do I have your permission," he said, leaning down enough so that she could feel the warmth of his breath on her cheek, "to use your weapons to hunt? I fear I cannot manage it with only my two hands."

She looked down at their joined fingers and swallowed hard. She tugged her hand gently from his grasp, severing the connection yet remaining at his side.

"Of – of course," she stammered. However foolish the agreement seemed, it was a chance she had to take. The man had not tried to harm her in any way; in fact, he had voluntarily held out his hands and let her tie him the night before. If he intended to steal her weapons or harm her, he could have easily done it while she was outside. She told herself it was the hunger that drove her and that the loneliness was getting to her, but the truth was that she believed him.

The rune mark scar on her palm ached as she closed her fingers into a fist. She made a mental note to be more careful about letting him see her hand. For the moment, she trusted him. If he saw her scar, that would be a different matter entirely.

They spent the next hour preparing to leave the cottage. As Daniel predicted, the snow seemed to be slowing down, and Emmy had to agree that it would not last much longer. While Daniel dressed, she looked longingly at her double layered winter parka shoved under her cot. She couldn't risk wearing it or having Daniel ask questions about the strange garment. Although it was still cold, the sun was starting to peek through the clouds, so she steadied her resolve to behave like a woman of her time should. She grudgingly donned her damp boots, lacing them up high enough to cover the thick cotton fleece socks she wore. Perhaps the layers would save her from the nip of frostbite. Her heavy wool cloak draped easily over her shoulders, and she welcomed the weight of the hood on her head. Although she would do everything she could to save the last two bullets in her gun, she tucked it securely in her belt anyway.

When she emerged, Daniel was waiting with the bow draped over his shoulder and a quiver of arrows on his back, and they set off on a path away from the cottage. There was a trail of boar tracks leading away from the house, pebbled with bits of dried corn husks and steaming piles of pig dung scattered along the way. *Maybe that damn boar was hunkered down nearby*, she mused.

They ran across good fortune when she spotted a hare in one of her traps behind a cover of dense fallen trees. It was frozen solid and there was no telling how long it has been there, but meat was meat and just seeing it made her mouth water. She'd been living on next to nothing since Connor left.

"Did you set this snare?" Daniel asked. She stood watch while he bent down and removed the rabbit from the wire. Daniel fumbled with the stiff wire for a moment until he figured out how it untwisted, and he looked up at her in question as he held up the contraption.

"My brother showed me how to do it. I haven't had a catch in about a week, though," she admitted. She watched as he bent the wire into a noose and reset the trap, and she offered him a length of twine which he wrapped around the rabbit's hind legs.

"I thought we might meet the boar first, with all the tracks nearby," Daniel said, tying the rabbit to his belt. Emmy glanced at the rabbit's dead eyes and quickly looked away. It was one thing to eat it, another thing entirely to see it looking like some kid's pet. Grateful for Daniel's company, she nodded in agreement.

"Last time it was near the cottage, I saw it had an ear-mark before I could get a shot at it. It probably belongs to someone," she replied.

"Well," he said, "I see no Englishmen here. All I see is a small woman with the look of hunger in her eyes."

"I'm not *that* small," she sniped. He chuckled, raising the edge of one dark brow.

"Small and mighty," he insisted. "I still cannot fathom how you dragged me so far. I am not nearly as small as you, and not so easy to move."

Snowflakes dappled his shoulders, leaving dark stains on the deerskin cloak he wore over his white tunic. The outline of a circular bloodstain was still on the fabric over his wound where she had mended his shirt, resistant to her efforts to scrub it clean. He looked like some sort of mythical warrior with the trim of fox hair lining the edge of his cloak and cradling his face, his dark eyes gleaming with humor as he gazed at her. She found a spot of comfort in the easy conversation, not minding so much that he teased her, only that he was there and that they shared the same space.

74

"It wasn't easy, but I managed," she said. She pointed to the creek bank about twenty yards away through the trees. "I found you over there. It wasn't that far."

He opened his mouth to reply, but before he could speak, they both heard the echo of shouts in the distance.

Her eyes darted towards the voices then back to Daniel, and her primary instinct was to run back to the cottage. Yet Daniel grabbed her hand and pulled her behind the dense fallen trees near the rabbit snare, shoving her down onto her knees in the snow. She was too startled to do anything but obey him, her blood running as frigid as ice through her veins when he enclosed her in his arms and burrowed halfway down beneath the cover of dead trees.

"Daniel?" she whispered. He squeezed her arm, shaking his head.

"Quiet. Let them pass," he ordered.

Snow was bunched up beneath her dress and in the crevices between her socks and boots, and as they burrowed down she could feel that the bottom of the trench was filled with icy water and they were sitting in it. She could scarcely breathe for want of his weight over hers and the unyielding circle of his arms. They were well hidden beneath the dense brush save for above their shoulders, and as long as the strangers did not venture off the path, they would not be discovered.

She nodded her acquiescence through her twinge of panic and he rubbed his thumb along her jaw in silent acknowledgment. There was no way for her to see anything but she suspected Daniel was watching. She struggled to slow her breathing, increasingly aware of the beat of Daniel's steady heart where her ear rested against his chest and the way his fingers twined in her damp hair. Snowfall already covered them, and although every inch of her skin burned with numbness, she was glad to see that their tracks were mostly hidden.

The voices drew closer; they spoke a language she did not understand. Daniel clamped his hand over her mouth, slowly shaking his head in warning.

6

Daniel

DANIEL HELD HER tighter than he intended, seeking to muffle her words by pressing her face into his shoulder. It was with some cajoling that Emmy submitted and he was relieved when she quieted. There was no telling what the men might do if they were discovered. Although he heard the cadence of their voices carry through the stillness of fresh fallen snow and he knew they were men of the First People, he could not decipher much until the men were close. By the time they were a dozen paces away, Daniel knew exactly who they were, and he could clearly hear what they spoke to each other in their Manahoac tongue.

"Ah, we should follow the water, and we will join the men by sundown," one of the men said, his thick voice clipped with annoyance. "We should not stay away from our people too long."

Daniel peered out through a gap in the branches and spotted a group of three men. Two of the men were stained with red and black vermillion and wore the scalp-lock style of warriors with a plucked scalp and a string of long braided hair trailing down their back. The third, however, was one who looked familiar to Daniel, and when the warrior turned and Daniel could see his profile, the identity of the man was clear.

Tall, lean, and garbed in the fur cloak of a War Chief, the man's sinewy muscles stood out like ribbons against his dark skin. He was tattooed across his forehead and upper lip, and his ears were pierced with curved copper rings and adorned with beads. His left eye was misshapen, bulging out from the socket as if it might burst, held back by a ragged flap of old scar tissue across his cheek and temple. When he spoke once more, Daniel recognized the Ricahecrian warrior. His voice betrayed his identity, more than the proud stature or defiant sneer on his face.

It was Wicawa Ni Tu – the man Daniel had promised the life of a Time Walker to.

Daniel shook off the memory and settled his grip firmer on Emmy. Yes, she knew enough to understand strangers were dangerous, and by the way she behaved he suspected she had a particular fear of Indians. Yet as much as Daniel had tried to gain her trust, it would be for naught if the Ricahecrians discovered them. There would be no mercy for him – or for her.

The Ricahecrian with the club standing above him would not spare him, and Daniel knew he would soon join his companions.

"Is he dead?" one of his enemies asked.

Daniel winced when the tip of a foot jabbed into his ribs.

"Not yet," another man answered. "Leave him. This is the one Wicawa Ni Tu wants. Let our Chief have the honor of ending his life."

Wicawa Ni Tu had every right to wish Daniel dead. After what had happened at the Falls, Daniel could not blame him for seeking vengeance.

"Perhaps the speaker perished in the river. He was gravely wounded when I left him," one of the men said. Wicawa Ni Tu glared at the man, his hard face etched with anger.

"You made the mistake of leaving him. I will not make the mistake of thinking him dead. A wounded man with nothing to lose makes for a fierce enemy," Wicawa Ni Tu said. "We will return to the village until the storm passes. If he lives, he will go to his family, and then we will find him."

The two others echoed their agreement with the plan.

Wicawa Ni Tu would go after his family. He might never tire of his thirst for vengeance, or his thirst to possess a powerful Blooded One. Sweat dappled Daniel's forehead despite the frigid forest air. Yet as he lay there in the snowy hollow beneath the fallen trees with Emmy clutched against his chest, Daniel no longer welcomed death. He knew it was coming – he knew exactly when it was coming – but suddenly he had something more to consider.

She was a mite of a woman, curled into his arms, warm breath on his skin and soft curves against his body, trying valiantly to stop herself from shuddering in the cold. She was a tumultuous spirit, brave at one moment and denying her fears the next. It was for her that suddenly he wanted to remain part of life, that he wanted to have a chance to change what the future might bring.

Was it honor that held him to this land? Or was it only the fear of the unknown that gripped him in those moments of release as he laid his head down to sleep each night? He knew what the Book of the Blooded Ones foretold of his lifetime, he had read it before he was yet a man. Although his Aunt Maggie tried to comfort him with tales of how the future might be changed, they both knew that his destiny was already decided.

Daniel pressed his lips into her hair. She remained silent. After a quarter of an hour where the men shared drinks from a flask and relieved themselves of their water, Wicawa Ni Tu barked a command at his companions and they set out on a path upriver closer to the creek. Despite the retreat, Daniel continued to hold Emmy for a long time, staring at the backs of the men as they left.

"They are gone," he finally said softly, his lips brushing the edge of her ear.

She did not object when he pulled her to her feet and brushed the snow from her hair. Her hood had fallen back and lay in a puddle around her neck, the darkness making the outline of her pale heart-shaped face and cherry-red cheeks stand out. He could see her breath in the air from her blue-tinged lips when she finally moved, a puff of mist exhaling as she relaxed in his embrace. When her teeth chattered, he grasped her hand and urged her back the way they had arrived. She was soaked through from the wet snow and frigid water they sheltered in. He was no better off, but it was only her that he could consider in light of how dire their situation might be.

"What if they follow us?" she whispered.

It pained him to explain. He did not want to think of what might have happened, nor envision what they might have done to her because of him.

"They went north along the river. It will take them away from us," he said, his voice hushed.

They were further from the cottage than he anticipated. What had once been large flakes of dusty snow became heavy icy pellets, striking their heads and coating them in dampness. His legs moved from pure strength of will, but she was beyond the grip of control and her feet lost purchase in the wet snow.

"I need to rest ... just for a few minutes," Emmy said, trying to weakly pull free from his grip. "I – I just need to sit down."

"No," he replied, jerking her back to him. Her knees buckled as if she meant to sit down but he swept her into his arms before she hit the snow. There was tearing sensation in his side as he lifted her which sent a stab of pain through his gut, yet he refused to dwell on that when she needed more from him.

If he did not get them back to the cottage, they would both die. She would succumb to the cold, and he would bleed out from his wound.

"Put me down," she murmured. He ignored her and kept walking, staggering at times in the deep snow. He kept off the deer trails, choosing to hide his tracks in the brush rather than risk anyone following them. Snowfall would cover them soon enough. As long as the Ricahecrians continued on their way north along the water, there was little chance of discovery.

When he finally arrived at the cottage, he brought Emmy inside and placed her gently down on her feet next to the fire. She clung to him but was relatively steady, hugging herself as she shuddered. Letting his cloak and the bow drop off of his shoulders in a heap by the fire, he threw a few dry logs on to stoke the flames and turned his attention back to her.

"I'm fine," she muttered, pushing at his hands when he unfastened her cloak. "I'm just cold."

"I know. You're soaked through. Turn around," he ordered. She followed his command without much protest and weakly gave him her back, allowing him access to unfasten her dress. He took the odd-shaped pistol from her belt and placed it on the hearth before he considered her dripping wet garments.

What kind of binding did she wear? He contemplated the way her dress was bound for a long moment, uncertain of the strange silver lace that held the thing together. There was a tab at the top which he discovered simply needed to be pulled, and seconds later the wet dress was gaping open. He parted it and pushed it down over her shoulders, letting it fall to a heavy heap on the floor. Her cotton chemise was soaked as well and needed to come off, and for all his honor as a man the act should not have stirred him, but it did. He untied it at her neckline and pulled it off over her head, immediately snatching a blanket and wrapping it around her naked body.

By the Gods, she was a vision. He could not help staring at her any more than he could stop taking a breath. What was it about her that drew him in, even from the first moment when he woke up tied to her bed? Was it her boldness, or the way she stood fiercely beside him with no care for her nakedness? Or was it the way she stared back at him, her soft eyes filled with a measure of trust? The longer he stayed in her presence, the stronger the pull, and despite the knowledge that he must soon leave, he wanted nothing more than to remain at her side.

His fate was already written. He had very little time left. Yet leaving her was suddenly something he could not do.

"Daniel?" she said softly. He shook his head as if it might quell his racing thoughts, trying to focus on putting more wood on the flames so that she might warm herself.

Emmy placed a hand on his arm and he slowly turned to face her, forgetting for the moment about tending the fire.

"You're freezing, too," she said. In truth, he felt only numbness over his skin, his damp garments sticking to his body. He sucked in his breath when she reached for his tunic, the simple graze of her fingertips on his flesh like a brand upon his skin. She raised the tunic and he elevated his arms, helping her tug it off over his head.

Her eyes suddenly lowered, and if he has not been so captivated by her he might have been pleased to see the flush rise to her cheeks when she reached to unfasten his breeches. He closed his hand over her fingers and dipped his head down, his cheek nearly brushing against hers and the sound of their rapid breaths loud in the space between them.

"Stand by the fire. Warm yourself," he urged her, his words choked through his dry lips. She nodded and turned to the fire, clutching the blanket around her shoulders without further protest.

He shed his breeches and used the blanket from his cot to cover himself, noting that there was a small amount of blood seeping through his bandage. It no longer pained him and he was not willing to worry on it until Emmy was taken care of.

"Thank you," Emmy said as Daniel joined her next to the fire. She was curled up on a fur, her knees tucked beneath her. Her long hair was starting to dry, a banner of loose tawny ringlets trailing down her back.

"Who were those men? Why did we need to hide?" she asked. He sat down beside her, stretching out his legs so that the heat of the flames licked his skin. Should he tell her the truth, or would it only cast more fear into her heart? She was clearly unsettled since her brother was gone, and Daniel had no idea if the man would ever return – or if he was alive at all. Even more pressing was the fact that Daniel knew he must leave and bring word of the slaughter at the Falls to the Pamunkey, but leaving Emmy was the last thing he wished to do.

"They are my enemies. If we were discovered, there would have been bloodshed," he answered. He bent slightly towards her, enough to catch the sweet scent of her damp hair. "And I feared I could not protect you ... not with this wound still fresh."

"I don't understand. Why would they want to harm us? I've met a few Indians since we've been here. None of them were any trouble," she replied. Daniel sighed. The only way to make her understand was to relive the truth.

"My uncle, Winn, was called to serve as a speaker for the Colonial Militia," Daniel said. The words were slow to surface, bringing back the images of the horrors in his mind. "My uncle refused. He is careful now about when he will serve the English, and even though Colonel Hill himself visited our home, Winn still refused him. I offered to go in his place."

"Your uncle sounds like an important man," Emmy said softly. Daniel nodded.

"He is. And I did not listen when he said I should not go," he replied. He felt her lean into him, shoulder to shoulder as they both stared into the flickering orange flames. She was starting to warm up and it seemed her tremors had stopped.

"Why did you do it? Help the English, I mean?" she asked.

It was a question that haunted him in his dreams, one that he could not put into words until that moment when Emmy asked it of him.

"I am half Paspahegh and half English. I thought if I could serve to quell the discord between the English and the First People, then my mixed blood would have meaning – some purpose. At Basse's Choice, I am an outsider. My Paspahegh kin are gone, and what ties I have to what remains of the Powhatan people are weak," he replied. He let his hand slip back around her, settling close enough so that his chin brushed the top of her head. "So I served the English. A group of First People settled on English lands not long ago, and the English Governor did not want them to stay. Colonel Hill was granted permission to settle the dispute. One hundred Pamunkey warriors joined the Militia, and I wished to support them. The English think that the land belongs to them, and only them, and that all others must have their permission to dwell upon it," he said. Emmy made a low snorting sound at that declaration.

"They do," she agreed. "I know what they've done to the First People."

It did not occur to him to question her meaning, so deeply caught in the tale of how he arrived in her care.

85

Perhaps the telling of it would silence the dreams; perhaps it would ease his anger.

"They are a mixed group of tribes. I think some are Tutelo, and some are Manahoac. The locals call them *Westos*. They were driven from their northern lands by the Iroquois. They only wish to live in peace, and I believed that I could help them come to some settlement with the English, like the Pamunkey have done.

When we arrived, five *Weroances* came to us and asked to speak to the English. Colonel Hill dispatched me to speak with the War Chief, *Wicawa Ni Tu*. While I spoke to *Wicawa Ni Tu*, Colonel Hill betrayed us all. He never intended to negotiate – he slaughtered the five Weroances in front of us. When they attacked, Colonel Hill and the Militia retreated, leaving the Pamunkey to fight alone."

"Daniel, you don't need to explain –" Emmy whispered.

"It did not take long," Daniel said quietly. "We were outnumbered. Every Pamunkey warrior was slaughtered. Even Totopotomoi, the Pamunkey Weroance and husband to my cousin, was killed. I should be among them as well. I should be one of the dead."

As the words left his lips, the memories of the battle echoed through his ears. He could feel it again, see it again, all of it. Every slain warrior in his path, every lost life. For what? The meaning of it all was buried in the ghost cries of the fallen that hammered in his ears every time he closed his eyes.

"I have never seen such a sight in all of my years. I have heard tales from my kinsmen, but until that day..." he let his words trail off. There was no need for her to know any more.

Emmy's hand slipped over his. She entwined her fingers with his and squeezed, allowing his arms to remain wrapped around her like a cocoon.

"You were not meant to die with them," she said.

"Was I not?" he countered. He knew it was foolish certainty of knowing the day of his death that led him to stand with the English. He regretted the touch of bitterness in his tone, despite the fact that it did not sway her. "Perhaps not. Now I must take the message to the Pamunkey, and I must tell my kinswoman that her husband is dead. She should hear it from my lips, since I was there to pay witness to it."

She did not reply but simply stayed close to him. He shifted a bit next to her, the feel of her in his arms giving him a measure of comfort. The smoky scent of burnt wood drifted to his senses and he reached out to push another log onto the flames.

"One of the men in the woods today was *Wicawa Ni Tu*. He thinks I betrayed him, that I led him into a trap. I did not stand to face him because you were with me. I was not fearful of meeting my fate then, nor am I afraid now ... but I would not have my fate fall on you."

Emmy turned to him, twisting around in his lap until her soft eyes met his. She placed her palm flat on his face, and he was frozen in place when she gently pressed her lips to his cheek.

"Thank you," she said. "Thank you for protecting me."

His throat suddenly felt dry, and the reality of his situation hammered into him like a blow to the chest. He was enjoying the comfort of a woman, when he should be making plans to return to the Pamunkey. He was losing himself in her presence, allowing her to fill that angry space in his soul that refused to submit. With her in his arms, he could easily ignore it all. He wanted to kiss her senseless; he wanted to lay her down beside the fire. Yet he needed to be better than that, he needed to be stronger. He left his home and his family to find his place in the world before his time expired. *What power did she hold over him, that he would throw away all care for the world for the chance to simply hold her?*

"I think ye are warm now, Miss Cameron," he said. He stood up and offered her his hand, which she took and allowed him to help her stand. Clutching the blanket at her neckline, she stared up at him for a long moment, lines creased at the edges of her green eyes and her mouth puckered slightly into a frown.

"I'm much better now," she agreed.

He could not stand the way she looked at him, eyes wide and full of questions, grateful and willing to stay in his arms. She was an English woman who had helped him live, and for that, he would be forever thankful. Yet she did not belong to him, and he had no right to think of dishonoring her by laying her down beside him, nor of taking her as a man might take his wife. His destiny was linked to the heart of another as foretold in the pages of the Book of the Blooded Ones, and for the first time in his life he deeply regretted ever knowing his future. And it was for that reason he would push away the urge to keep her in his arms.

"I am glad," he replied. He retrieved her pistol from the hearth and pressed it into her hand. "You should rest. Take your sleep, and I will stay up a bit to keep watch. I will keep the candle burning for you."

"All right," she said. "Good night, then."

She disappeared behind the drape, leaving him alone to face the chaos in his mind.

No matter. In the morning, things would make more sense. His thoughts would clear, the wound in his side would be improved, and he would decide on a plan to do what he needed to do.

7

Emmy

THE SCENT OF roasted meat woke her from her sleep, making her stomach rumble in the most uncomfortable way. She slipped out of bed dressed only in her white cotton chemise and peered around the edge of the drape, noting the empty cottage and that Daniel's cot seemed unused.

"Daniel?" she called out. Her dress was still damp when she checked but her cloak was dry, so she pulled the cloak around her shoulders and went to investigate. On the hearth, a fresh pot of stew was brewing, and when she checked the scrap bucket she saw the remnants of a white-tailed hare.

"Smells delicious," she muttered. Tying the cloak at the base of her neck, she glanced out the window. The snowfall had stopped, replaced by the warmth of early morning sunshine in the clearing. Outside, Daniel was chopping wood. Apparently he had found the rusted ax in the rubbish pile by the storage shed. It was ungainly enough for her to wield, but he seemed to be doing fine with it despite his injury.

Quite fine, in fact. So much so that every time he raised the ax above his head and struck, the outline of his taut muscles stood out like cords on his arms. He was focused on his task, his long dark hair tied back but falling over one shoulder as he worked.

For all she had ever known of history, she could never have imagined that men like him lived in the past. It was one thing to study history, and another thing entirely to *live* it. She was not unmoved by what he had done for her, and it caused her a considerable amount of guilt to recall that she had been willing to kill him rather than help him when she found him wounded by the creek. Looking at him now and knowing that he had likely saved her life, he had become much more to her than some stranger.

She shoved her feet into her damp boots and went out to meet him. When she opened the plank door he immediately stopped, pausing his work by impaling the ax on the flat stump he used as a base for cutting. Wiping the sweat from his brow with the back of his forearm, he rested one hand on the end of the ax handle and met her curious gaze with a nod.

"I would have done that. I still have enough left for a few days," she said, stammering the words out. She wasn't completely helpless, and she'd be damned if she couldn't chop her own wood, but she still felt the need to chastise him.

"Oh, you've been cutting it yourself?" he asked, a wry grin edging his lips.

She scowled. Truthfully, she had not cut any of the wood, it was actually what Connor had cut before he left. However, that did not mean she *couldn't* do it, and it annoyed her to no end that Daniel thought so little of her ability to take care of herself.

Marching up to him, she cocked an eyebrow at him and held out her hand. He uttered a low chuckle and gave her the ax, holding his arm out in a sweeping gesture of submission.

"For you, Miss Cameron," he said graciously.

"Hmpf," she snorted. She shoved her cloak off her shoulders and then snatched the ax and raised it over her head, shooting him a sideways glare before she concentrated on the wood. It was only a small piece. How difficult could it be?

She brought the ax down with all of her might, completely missed the log she meant to split, and buried the head of the ax into the stump. Daniel burst into a fit of laughter which only served to heighten her frustration as she tried to wrench the ax from the stump without success.

"Damn it!" she cursed. She shoved at him when he tried to take the ax from her, but he was persistent and took hold of it despite her resistance.

"Let me –" he offered.

"No! I've got it!" she insisted.

Hands entwined on the handle, they both yanked at the same time, sending them tumbling to the ground in a heap while the ax flew off into the snow a few feet away. His body slammed into hers with an audible thump and the wind rushed from her lungs in protest. Despite the effort to breathe while pinned down like a pancaked snow angel, she joined him in his amusement with laughter of her own.

It felt good to laugh. Even if he was smothering her.

"Pray tell me," Daniel asked, seeming to hold his laughter in check for a moment. "How did you cut all that wood?"

Emmy bit back a giggle. "I didn't. Connor cut it. But I could have if I had to!"

Daniel grunted a half-laugh, half-snort. He pushed himself up on one elbow, his face entirely too close to hers. Suddenly she was acutely aware of the way her body fit into his, curved and tangled in a way that brought a rush of warmth over her now numb and wet skin.

"Of course," Daniel agreed, his voice hoarse. She could see in his eyes that he was just as affected as she was, and when she shifted slightly beneath him, his gaze met hers. His throat contracted and his eyes darted downward to where her damp shift was sticking to her skin and her breasts were pressed against his chest, then back upward, where his gaze lingered on her lips for a long moment before meeting her eyes once more.

"I can take care of myself," she said, her voice no more than a whisper.

"Of that, I have no doubt," he replied.

Her heart was pounding like a drum and the warmth of his breath on her cheek sent a blaze of fire through her bones. When he bent his head next to her ear she bit into her lower lip and closed her eyes.

"You should go back inside before you freeze," he simply said, drawing back. He rolled to his side and sat up in the snow, running his hands through his hair before he looked back at her.

A bit out of breath and thoroughly warm despite her soaked shift, she sat up beside him. He handed her the cloak she had dropped on the ground, averting his eyes from hers.

"I'm sorry. I must have crushed you," he finally said.

"It's okay. I'm fine," she insisted. "I really can take care of myself, I assure you." A part of her wanted to ask if she had imagined the entire thing, or if he had felt it too, yet the practical side of her took control and dismissed her scattered girlish thoughts.

"I see that," he replied, his words careful and even. "But I think another storm is coming soon, and you will need more wood after I leave. You should go inside before a chill catches you again. I'll finish here."

Her response stuck in her throat. *He was going to leave.* Of course he was; what else did she expect him to do? She silently berated herself for imagining anything else. He had a life to return to, a duty to fulfill, the same as she did. It was high time she started getting herself in order to do the same.

He stood up and offered her his hand, which she took. He did not linger, immediately grabbing the ax and returning to the last of the wood. She stood there and watched him for a long moment, clutching her arms over her chest, and finally the cold numbness hit her and she retreated back into the cottage.

Get your shit together, Emelia Leigh Cameron, she thought. *Stop acting like some attention-starved teenager.* Daniel was a momentary distraction in the greater scheme of things; she had a duty to her mother and brother to make it to Smithfield before April, even if Connor never returned. It was what she was born to do. She was a Blooded One, and her future would be lived in the past.

She went into the cottage and quickly changed into her dress, annoyed that it was still slightly damp, which made the layers of cotton heavy and unmanageable. Her shift was soaked through and she should have been mortified, but she was too irritated and wound up to consider it much. She had plenty of other things to keep her attention, namely, the stew that was boiling over on the fire.

Daniel came inside with an armful of wood, which he deposited in a pile next to the hearth. She kept busy stirring the stew, and although she tried not to care too much what he was doing, she could not help but notice him pull his tunic off over his head across the room. He took up one of Connor's white linen shirts that she had given him and placed his wet garment near the fire to dry.

"You know, I have somewhere I need to be, the same as you do," she said. The attempt at making casual conversation was more of a confirmation for her, as if she needed to prove something to him – or to herself.

"Oh, do you?" he replied, sitting down at the small table in the middle of the room. His shirt was gaping open and he was examining his bandage, his dark brows furrowed downward, as if he did not care at all for what she was talking about.

"Yes. I'm going to Smithfield. I – I have important business there."

"I know no Smithfield. Is it an English town?" he replied.

She frowned, stirring the stew a bit more irately. "Of course it is. I mean, it's downriver, not far from Jamestown. You must have heard of it."

He cocked his head slightly sideways to look at her. "I cannot keep track of every English town, as they have spread in number throughout *Tsenacommacah* each year. If you say it is a town, then I believe your words, Miss Cameron."

She didn't know why his response infuriated her, or why it made her feel so frigid when he held their tenuous relationship to propriety and called her Miss Cameron.

"Well, that's where I need to go. I suppose we can both leave at the same time then."

"If you wish," he replied.

They ate together mostly in silence, and the rest of the afternoon was no better. In the days that she had taken care of Daniel before he woke up, she had spent the time searching for her brother or busied herself around the cottage with various chores and had never seemed to need to find ways to pass the hours. Since Daniel woke, however, her entire world was in a tailspin. The mundane activities no longer satisfied her, and her impatience with her situation grew stronger every moment. If she were being truthful to herself, she knew it was because of the conflict of what she was meant to do colliding with the reality of the situation before her.

It was easy to let Daniel's presence distract her, rather than face the idea of traveling alone, or, for that matter, where to travel to. Although Connor made her promise to get to Smithfield no matter what happened, could she do that if it meant abandoning hope of ever finding him?

Leave and never see Connor again, or disobey him and go to the Ricahecrian trading village in search of him?

Regardless of her decision, neither option was one she could live with.

Emmy drifted over to the window, noticing a flash of movement outside. At first she thought it was some sort of dog, but when she rubbed her fist on the foggy window to clear the glass, she realized it was a large, dark feathered turkey.

"Daniel!" she said, her excitement spilling over as she ducked away from the window and grabbed the bow leaning up against a nook in the wall. She scrambled to shove her feet into her boots and grabbed the door, searching through a flurry of her tangled hair and clothes to thread an arrow on the bow.

Emmy darted out the door before Daniel responded. Thankfully, the turkey was not too much repelled by the creak and clatter of the opening door, and Emmy was thrilled to see it was not just one bird, but a small flock of about a dozen. Most of them were near the wood line and sheltered by the dense brush, but the one she had spotted from the window stood in the clearing near the chopping block stump, his thick dark body outlined against the melting snow. It looked to be a male, larger and darker colored than the brown females, and he had a bright red wattle hanging from his puckered neck.

She widened her stance and drew the arrow back, aware that the Indian short bow was much lighter than the compound archery bow she had taken her lessons on, yet it released swift and straight and found the target. As the arrow pierced the breast of the turkey and it fell to the ground, memories of the time spent in preparation for that moment rushed back to her.

"But I don't want to shoot it," she whispered to Connor. They were crouched down behind a wall of straw bales, looking upon a spotted doe that was munching on the budding leaves of a young sugar maple sapling. The wildlife in the hunting preserve was plentiful, and although they had come there that day with the intent of sharpening her skills, Emmy still did not want to do it. After all, it was her tenth birthday, and she shouldn't have to kill an animal if she didn't want to.

"Do it, Emmy. You have to do it," Connor demanded. "You have to learn how to take care of yourself, no matter what time you're in. I won't always be there to do it for you."

She fought back the surge of tears as she glared at her brother. He swore when she threw her bow into the dirt and stalked away from him, her motion sending the deer darting off into the woods and scattering a nearby flock of birds up into the trees.

"I don't care where you and mother try to send me – I'm not going!" she shouted, yanking her archery gloves off and throwing them at her brother for good measure. "I'm staying here, in this time, and you can't make me leave!"

Connor's face hardened, his skin flushed bright red while he picked up her bow. Her stomach twisted into a knot when he grabbed her bow and stalked over to her, his fury blazing across his features. She gritted her chin and held her ground, expecting some sort of retaliation, and was stunned when he simply thrust the bow back into her hands.

"You'll end up where you're meant to be, no matter what any of us do. Better to be prepared for what you will face, then to end up some helpless fool stuck in the past," *he said, his voice low and even. "Now put your gloves back on and get that bow ready."*

Emmy notched another arrow to the bow and drew it back as she approached the turkey, ready for a second shot if it was not dead. She gave the bird a tap with her toe, and when it did not move she lowered her weapon.

"I got it," she called out, swinging around to show off her kill to Daniel. She was too engrossed with thoughts of having a hearty meal to notice that Daniel was coming towards her quite quickly, and it was not until he was a few feet away that she noticed the knife positioned in his raised hand. His gaze was not on her, but focused beyond her, a mask of pure ferocity etched on his face.

"Daniel?" she said, confused. The trees behind her rustled and a grove of cat-tailed reeds parted, and she saw the man just as Daniel released his knife. The blade sailed past her face before she could utter a word, impaling into the man's chest and bringing him down. His body crashed into Emmy and they fell to the ground in a heap. The wind was knocked from her lungs and she could feel the warmth of something sticky on her face and neck, and when she gasped and tried to scramble away from the man, the bitter metal taste of blood filled her mouth.

"No," she cried out, "No!"

It was a reflexive plea uttered from her stunned lips, more of a denial than a request. She shrieked when the man moved and his fingers gripped at her neck, yet suddenly the weight of his body was thrust away.

Daniel held the man by his throat and the man weakly tried to grab Daniel. Stunned, Emmy sat up and scrambled backward, choking and sputtering for air, the horror of the bleeding man leaving her frozen in place. Daniel shouted at him in a language she could not decipher, eliciting no response from the stranger except for a defiant grin over bloody teeth.

Who was the stranger and what had he done? She gasped when Daniel stabbed him, ending the last throes of his life with a swift stab to the neck. As much as she thought she could take the life of another if necessity called for it, the reality of killing a man was quite another when she was staring it straight in the face. Yes, she had been trained by her brother to be fierce and calculated when protecting herself, yet nothing in her twenty-first-century training could have truly prepared her for it.

Daniel lowered his head, turning slightly towards her at the sound. His chest heaved and she could see the tense lines carved in his face, noting that he held the bloody knife down at his side for a long moment while he stood over the man.

"Why – why did you – who was that man?" Emmy stammered. When Daniel took a pace towards her, she cringed, and she did not miss the hardness in his eye at her motion.

"He was a scout," he replied. "And he had his weapon aimed at you."

Emmy swallowed hard. A rush of coldness hit her, and suddenly the reality of where she was and what she was doing felt like a heaviness in her gut. Daniel was right; beside the fallen stranger was a long hunting knife.

So wrapped up in her hunting prowess, she had not seen the man who had almost killed her. If not for Daniel, she would be dead.

"Daniel, I –"

"Tend to your catch," Daniel said, his words short and crisp. "I will deal with this and join you soon."

He turned away from her, putting space between them. With no sense of what she should say to him and a shadow of utter confusion holding her, she wiped the blood from her face with the back of her hand and bent to the task of preparing the turkey.

There was no time for regret or fear, or any other indulgent emotion. Daniel was steady and sure, straight as the ancient cypress trees reaching for the sky. He did what he had to do to survive, just as she must learn to do, and losing her shit over one dead man and a little blood on her skin was not how she was raised to behave.

I'm fine, she told herself. *I'm absolutely fine.*

IT TOOK HER an hour to butcher the bird, but it yielded a considerable amount of meat. Most of it she wrapped in linen and stored outside in the bank of snow; it would keep there until she could slice it and set it out in the sun to dry. Since they still had a decent amount of rabbit stew, she figured it was better to make the turkey meat more portable in preparation for traveling. Afterward she scrubbed the blood from her skin with a cold washcloth.

Blood from men and animals looked exactly the same.

Daniel did not come inside until after it was dark. He sat down at the table without a word, taking a long swallow of the cider she set out for him. He was freshly washed and she wondered if he had bathed outside, her own skin covered in goosebumps at the thought. She tried to tear her gaze away from him, but she was confused by his coldness and at a loss for what to say to him. *Was he angry at her? Or was it something else?*

She set a bowl of food down in front of him and turned away, shocked when he reached out and closed his hand over her wrist.

"Are you all right?" he asked.

She nodded, eager to quell the distance between them.

"Of course. I'm fine," she replied, her voice wavering. "You did what had to be done." *And I've just realized that maybe I am not strong enough to do the same, and maybe I was never truly prepared to live in this time, and it terrifies me,* she wanted to add.

He stood up, keeping hold of her hand, and raised it to his cheek. She flattened her palm against his skin, meeting his steady gaze as he looked down on her.

"I took the life of a man today, and I will carry that with me for all of my days, just as I carry the stain of the battle upon my spirit," Daniel said, his voice low. She could see the turmoil inside him as clear as she felt her own. "Yet carrying that with me is nothing, if I must bear the burden of your fear. I saw it in you when you looked at me, when it was done. I see it now in you, just as I feel you tremble at my touch since the day we met. Tell me, what was done to you, so that I can banish it from your thoughts."

She stared back at him, the words caught on her dry lips. She wanted to tell him everything, tell him all of it – how she was not from his time and how her kind had been hunted like animals, or how she knew the truth of what would someday happen to them all. That he was raw, and instinctive, and fiercely strong, and that he sometimes took her breath away with the hint of a glance. That he frightened her and she hated to feel fear, or that he was something she could not control and that terrified her even more.

"I'm not afraid of anything," she whispered instead, leaving the truth unsaid. "I thank you for what you did." She could hear the pounding of her pulse in her ears as he lowered his head, his lips only inches from hers.

"You saved my life once. I will never let harm come to you," he said softly. She stiffened at his declaration, both inflamed by the way their bodies melded so closely together and angered by the implication of duty in his words.

"Because of duty, then?" she asked, breathless.

"No," he replied, his gaze shifting to her lips. "Duty is not what I want between us."

His mouth closed over hers and he threaded his fingers into her hair, drawing her body into his. She arched up against him, shocked by the firmness of his touch, as if he expected what was between them as some foregone conclusion. Gentle at first, his lips covered hers, searching and seeking, his tongue brushing hers and drawing a whispered moan from her.

What was he doing to her, and why did any of it matter? She gladly lost the edge of fear she carried, welcoming his touch when he backed her up against the wall. He smothered that flame of despair in her heart, his embrace enough to chase the demons away and still the pace of racing time.

She had been kissed before, but never with the brand of possession he placed upon her. Every inch of her skin was on fire, aching to follow the siren call of his lips, loving the way she could feel his hard desire against her belly through the layers of their clothes. She shifted

103

her hips, fitting closer to him, and he let out a low groan against her mouth.

He drew back from her then, the crackle of the fire and the sound of their ragged breaths filling the space as they stared at each other.

"'Tis not duty, *eholen*," he said softly. He let her go and she stayed upright against the wall, her limbs weak like a limp rubber band and her heart hammering in her chest. She closed her eyes when he kissed her gently on her forehead and then turned away. She opened them as he left, and she watched him close the door of the cottage securely behind him.

Later, when the glow of moonlight streamed through the window and she lay awake in her bed, she heard him come in. His bed ropes creaked, accepting his weight as he laid down, and Emmy closed her eyes.

If it was this time that she was meant for, then what part did Daniel play in it? She drifted off with the memory of his lips on her skin, and for the first time in her life she prayed to the Gods of men for an answer.

8

Daniel

HE WANTED TO run, but the wound in his side made it impossible for him to stand. He could hear the screams of his fellow warriors as he dragged himself through the deep mud, and he was ashamed that he could not stand up to face his enemy.

The glow of the setting sun sifted through the trees, illuminating the body of a warrior impaled to a tree. His limbs were twisted and bloodied, but when Daniel looked at him, his dead eyes opened wide and his ghostly mouth uttered a whispered command.

"Run," the dead man said. *"Hurry."*

"Daniel?"

He woke from the dream with a start, feeling hands press on his cheeks. He could still hear the cries of the fallen and smell the scent of death in his nostrils. At first he thought it was the touch of a ghost and he tried to push it away, but the grip was persistent and soon Emmy came into focus. He looked at her through glazed vision, his breath coming in short spurts. Despite the sweat dripping from his skin, she held on tightly, until his breathing had slowed enough to quell the panic in his soul.

"You were moaning in your sleep," she said. "It must have been a dream."

Her hair was loose, hanging tousled around her heart shaped face. In the dim shadows of the firelight he could see the worry in her eyes. The harsh truth of his nightmare ebbed away, but in its place there was the edge of something raw that still made him cling to her, and it urged his hands upward to cradle her face until his fingers were entwined in her hair.

She was tense, unmoving, her jade eyes locked with his. He didn't know why he did it, only that he could not stop himself this time, and when his lips sought hers it was the warmth of her that kept him tied to the earth. Be it the remnants of the dream or the simple weakness of his restraint as a man, he needed to taste her.

He wanted her. Destiny be damned, he burned for her, and by the Gods, he would deny it no longer. She let out a soft cry as he pulled her down and kissed her, but he was not yet satiated of his need.

Holding her in his arms tethered him to the living; feeling her body soften and meld to his touch was the power that chased the ghosts away. If he could only keep her close, let her be the master of him, then he could lose himself in the blessed depths of surrender without regret. He let out a low groan when her hand slipped behind his neck, the simple gesture of submission enough to spiral him past control and bury the last vestige of his honor. He pulled her close and covered her body with his, pinning her to the mattress beneath him.

"Daniel?" she whispered. His lips left hers, tracing a path down the curve of her cheek and then lower to the hollow of her throat. When he pushed his hand inside her shift against her silken skin and cupped her round breast, she arched up to meet his touch and moaned his name again, driving him to utter madness with desire pounding in his chest.

"Do not ask me to stop," he said, breathing the words hotly against her skin. He closed his mouth over the tight peak, loving the way she tossed her head back and clutched his head to her breast.

"Please don't stop," she cried.

By the Gods, he thought, *what power does this woman wield?* He was glad to service her, hungry to hear her moan, aching with every ounce of his blood to hear her scream his name. It was that task that drove him to wait, taking his time to see to her pleasure before he took his own. Whatever power brought them together, it was that moment that made it clear, and when he gripped her hips and she writhed up beneath his hungry mouth and cried his name, he knew tasting her was as close to the afterworld as he might ever be while he still lived.

She was still shaking when he moved up and settled between her legs, her eyes half opened but locked on his. He felt the control slip from his grasp as he stared down at her, and although he feared he might hurt her, she urged him on. She kissed him hard and he wrenched her hands up above her head, pinning them to the mattress, seeking to still her for the moment before he ravaged her.

His fingers brushed the flat opened palm of her left hand. Upon her skin was a thick healing wound, which he glanced briefly at and then froze. Slowly, his gaze flickered back to hers. In the gleam of the firelight her jade eyes widened, and he could see the panic rush into her face. Between them they sought to catch their breath, staring at each other in silence. He did not want to be the one to say the words, yet clearly, she was waiting for him to react.

"Time Walker," he said softly, his lips still close to hers as the implication roared through his mind. He expected her to react in some way, but he did not expect her to attack him. She tried to break the grip he had on her hands, elbowing him in his jaw in her struggle and grinding her naked hips against his as she tried to squirm away from him, but he knew that if he let her go now, she would never listen to him.

A Time Walker? Of course it was possible, yet still, the knowledge of who she was startled him. All of her uncertainty, all of her fears, suddenly made sense. Her strange behavior, her boldness, her peculiar speech – because she was born to another time. It fell into place in an instant, the prediction of his future and the Time Walker who was destined to belong to him, suddenly living and real and in his arms. Was she blood kin to his Aunt Maggie in some way? What time was she from? Despite his questions, Emmy was clearly not prepared to offer any answers. In fact, she was fighting like an angry badger to get away from him, when all he wanted to do was quell her doubts.

"Let go of me!" she shouted, her eyes panicked. She bucked up beneath him and he swore an oath, still wanting nothing more than to bury himself inside her and settle the matter of where she was from at a later time.

"Stop your struggle, unless you wish to finish what we started," he shot back, his frustration surging to the surface. He let loose of her hands and instantly regretted his decision when she snatched her gun from the stool next to his bed. The realization that she still carried the weapon everywhere she went was not lost on him.

"Let me up," she demanded, pressing the gun to his chest. He drew back slightly, glancing down at the weapon and then back to her eyes, shaking his head. It was clear that Emmy had no idea of who he was, nor what path they were foretold to travel together.

"You saved me for a reason, Emmy. Was it only to take my life by your own hand?" he said softly. Her rapid breathing was loud in the silence. He longed to wrap his arms around her and prove his intentions, yet a part of him was shaken to the core by the revelation of who she was.

"You don't understand," she whispered.

He slowly sat up, letting her have the comfort of her weapon for a few more moments until he snatched it from her hands. She jumped away from him, shrinking back on the bed into the corner of the wall, as if she feared he might use the gun on her.

She thinks I am the enemy now. He rested his head in his hand, leaning on his knees to process the truth screaming between his ears. *But I know who she is – and I know what she is to me.*

"Your given name is Emelia Leigh," he finally said, his voice low. "And you are a Blooded One."

She shifted in the bed, sitting up and forward on her knees. Not quite touching him, but not cowering, so he considered her motions and let a shadow of hope rest in his thoughts.

"How do you know that?" she asked. "Who are you?"

Daniel held the gun out to her, meeting her gaze.

"I read it in a book," he replied. "A book that should not be read by the eyes of the living."

She took the gun, but did not point it at him, instead letting it fall into her lap.

"The *Leabhar Sinnsreadh*," she answered. "The Book of the Blooded Ones. But only the Chief Protector holds the book. One of the Five ... one of the Five Northman."

The realization of the connection streamed across her face. He nodded. "In this time, 'tis the Neilsson Chief that holds it. My Uncle Winn, to be exact."

"That's not possible," she insisted, shaking her head. She looked dangerously close to losing her senses with her teeth biting into her lower lip, shaking so hard he thought she might make herself bleed.

He took a chance and reached for her, hoping that the connection between them was not completely lost. She was like a plank in his arms but he persisted, encircling her with his embrace until her body finally relaxed with a long sigh. The fight left her for the moment, and he was grateful for the interlude.

"There's no record of Norsemen in this time," she whispered. She banged her closed fist on his chest to enunciate her point, and he could feel the cold metal of the gun against his bare shoulder where she held it in her other hand. "They left no trace. There is nothing in the history books about them."

"Nor would there be. My Aunt and Uncle take great pains to stay hidden. Even the village where I was born was burned to the ground to hide what life we had lived there," he replied.

"So they're in hiding, just like we were our entire lives."

He nodded. "'Tis safer for all of us that way." He leaned back against the wall, taking her with him as he was unwilling to break their tentative bond. She was afraid, and from what he knew of how her kind had suffered, he could not blame her for it. Yet for all her knowledge of what she was, she clearly did not know what she was *to him* – and she was in no way ready for him to reveal it to her.

"Are you – are you like me? A Blooded One?" she asked.

"No. My father's life was once saved by my cousin, who is like you. I was not born of your kind, but they are my kin, and I know what it means to bear that blood."

"My brother said to trust no one. I don't know what to think. I'm supposed to be in Smithfield, but it's not just chance that you're here. I – I wasn't prepared for any of this," she insisted.

"You are here because you are meant to be here. I am here because you saved my life. That is what was meant to happen," he said. "And when you go, I will go with you."

She pulled slightly away, her searching gaze locking on his.

"Why? You don't owe me anything. It's not your duty, it's mine."

"When I was young, I read the book. I wish I did not, but it is not something that can be undone. When I say I will accompany you, it is because that is what my future holds."

"So this – all of this – you're only doing it because what that book says?" she asked. Her words wavered, the softness in her eyes shadowed in hurt.

"No," he replied, his voice low and hoarse. "I need no book to tell me what I want, or where I will go. Yes, it is written, but the choice is mine."

Daniel took her hand and turned it over, pressing her scarred palm gently to his lips. The burn for her was still there, dimmed slightly by the sudden truth between them, yet it was strengthened by it all the same. *She belonged to him. She was his beginning, his life, and his end. And she did not know it yet.*

"Take your rest, *eholen*," he said softly, pledging his soul to her in words she could not understand. She did not know what it meant, but soon, he would ensure that she did. "Keep your weapon if it calms you. Be safe here in my arms until the sun rises, and then we will see what greets us."

He felt her throat contract as she swallowed hard and ducked her head into his shoulder. *Was it sheer exhaustion, or did she trust him?* He had no notion, but for now, it was enough.

They spoke softly together for some time. He listened to stories of her future world, and she asked him many questions about the Time Walkers he called kin. She struggled to make sense of it all, sharing with him the tale of how she grew up always knowing that her destiny was in the past, and that when she was of age she would travel through time to satisfy it. She was trained to survive and schooled in history and medicine, yet Daniel could clearly see that she did not know who he was.

Was it for him to tell her, or was it something she should discover of her own free will? Part of him wanted to tell her, to make her understand – and then to lay her down and finish making her his own. Yet as badly as his desire still burned, the honor he felt towards her was just as strong, and he knew it was a truth she must discover with time.

Soon her tired eyes closed and he felt her breathing slow to an easy rhythm. The rest of the conversation they must have would wait, and for that he was thankful.

"Daniel?" she murmured, clutching her fist to his chest.

"Yes?"

"The light," she said. "Keep the candle burning. Please."

He glanced at the half-burned candle in the glass globe lantern at his bedside. It would last a few more hours, at least, and likely until sunrise, but if it was what she needed to sleep in peace, then he would gladly give it to her.

"I will," he replied. He felt her nod.

Although she drifted off into a fitful sleep not long afterward, he stayed awake, taking comfort in the feel of her warm skin against his.

Mine, he thought. *For the time that we have, she is mine.*

HE WOKE WITH the rising of the sun the next morning. He slept little during the night, watching over Emmy through her restless dreams and wishing to protect her from all that was to come. She did not know yet what part she played in his life, and for all truth, the knowledge of it startled him to the core. Yet with the acceptance of knowing who she was came a harsh truth;

he also knew her brother – and he knew her brother was likely dead.

There was no other explanation; the Time Walker prisoner of the Ricahecrians was her missing brother. He had no notion of how it happened, or how long the man had been held captive, but from the glimpse of the blond-haired man's features it was clear he was kin to Emmy. Even if the man had survived the battle, he surely would be dead by now from the bloodletting. Just exactly how he was going to tell her was another matter, as was the fact that Wicawa Ni Tu sent a scout looking for him and that they needed to leave soon if they wished to live.

And that Daniel had promised Wicawa Ni Tu the life of the captive's family – the Time Walker woman who lay sleeping in his care.

He sat down on the edge of his bed, careful in his motion so as not to wake her, for he wished to look upon her for a time without that truth haunting her thoughts. Her eyes were closed gently in sleep, her hair fanning out on the pillow beneath her head like the crescent of a shimmering sun. The laces of her shift lay open, exposing her soft pale skin, and he wanted badly to trace his lips down the sweet curve of her neck and breast to where her plum-colored nipple peaked under the thin fabric. She shifted, her hand reaching out to him, and he was immediately stirred when her fingers slipped along his thigh. By the Gods, he wanted her, and he doubted that his thirst would ever dim.

"Morning," she whispered, opening her eyes with the hint of a shy sleepy smile. She sat up slightly and reached to fasten her gown, but he caught her hand and pressed her fingers to his lips.

"No, leave it," he said, not yet ready to stop gazing at her. She did not protest when he slowly parted her shift, letting it fall loosely down her shoulders so that she was bared to him. He knew that for the rest of his days he would always picture her that way, flushed and breathless, her eyes locked with his, the soft curves of her rounded breasts naked for him.

"Stop looking at me like that," she said.

"Never," he replied, drawing her to him. He kissed her hard, feeling her tight nipples pressed against his chest and needing with every ounce of his blood to finish what they had started the night before. He gripped her bottom with one hand and pulled her onto his lap, letting her legs fall open around him, fumbling with his breeches to free himself, yet the moment was shattered by the sound of the door crashing open.

Emmy let out a muffled scream as his cousin, Ahi Kekeleksu, burst into the dwelling, his flint-lock musket aimed and ready to fire at them. The Paspahegh brave lowered his weapon once he surveyed the scene before him, an irritated scowl edging his face.

"I see you are not dead yet," Keke said, slinging the musket over his shoulder. Emmy scrambled to cover herself, darting beneath the covers while Daniel stood up. "But you *will* be if you stay here any longer. I spotted a Ricahecrian hunting party upstream, and I fear there are more to come." He tipped his head leisurely to Emmy, as if his intrusion was as normal as the rising sun. "My lady," he murmured.

Daniel pulled his tunic over his head and shoved his feet into his boots, holding his hand out to Emmy.

"Hurry. Pack what you can. My cousin speaks true – there will be more," Daniel said.

Emmy stood up, but he could see that she was shaking. He was unsettled as well, but they had no time to dwell on it or to question Ahi Kekeleksu. Another band of Ricahecrians so soon after the last was reason enough to leave. Later, when they were alone and safe, he would explain the rest of it to her.

"You said the *Ricahecrians*," she spoke. "I *know* them. They're friendly – I've been to their village to trade. They might know where my brother is – I need to ask them if they've seen him!"

His blood seemed to drain from his heart as rising panic took over. *He needed to get her away.* He needed to take her far away from the Ricahecrians. There was nothing on earth that would keep him from that task.

"They are the tribe we fought at the Falls. They are slave traders, and they are our enemy," Daniel replied, his voice firm. "You will *not* stay. You will go with us."

"It's not your decision to make," she shot back.

Daniel ignored Keke's snort, aware that they had no time to argue and incensed that she refused him. *Did she not see the danger before them? Must he say the words that would hurt her, in order to save her life?*

Daniel placed his hands on her shoulders, holding her firmly so that she might listen. She stared defiantly up at him, green eyes blazing, her lips braced in a tight thin line.

"Get dressed, or go as you are, but be assured, you *will* go with us," Daniel intoned.

"No, I won't," she replied.

He squeezed her then, hard, and refused to let her pull away.

"Yes, *you will*," he ground out, his voice low and coarse. "I saw your brother during the battle. He was a prisoner of Wicawa Ni Tu. They will kill you if you go to them. They will never let him go!"

Emmy let out a cry and wrenched free, and this time he let her go. Daniel hated himself in that moment as he fired defiance back at her, showing her that there was no question she would evade his order. He snatched her dress from her bed and shoved it into her shaking hands.

"No," she whispered. "I can't just leave him like that. I can't!"

"He is as good as dead. There is no reason for you to stay. Gather your things, we are leaving." The cold words were his own, but he felt far removed from his own voice, hating the harshness and hating himself. If he had to choose between the possibility of saving a dead man or ensuring Emmy lived, then he would choose her life every time, brother or not.

Tears streamed down her face as she pushed past him and went across the room to her space, ducking behind the drape. He could see she was shoving things into her satchel, so he left her to her own devices for the moment while he turned to his cousin.

"Who is the woman?" Keke asked, his voice low.

"She is Emelia Leigh, and she is mine," Daniel replied. It was all the explanation that Keke needed. His cousin knew the tale of Daniel's future and there was no further question.

"Ah, she is a tiny thing for a Time Walker, but I think she might kill you if she gets the chance," Keke said. Daniel grimaced, knowing there was some truth to his cousin's words.

"Not yet, cousin. 'Tis not the time," Daniel replied. He finished dressing in layers and grabbed the short bow, slinging it over his shoulder with the quiver of arrows. Emmy emerged, dressed with her fur-lined cloak over her dress and her odd-shaped satchel hanging from her arm, her long hair gathered with a ribbon to one side of her neck. Her red-rimmed eyes seemed to stare through him, her features a strained mask, and he could see the handle of her gun tucked into her belt.

"I'm ready," she said. She walked past both of the men and left the door open, trudging out into the cold as she clutched her belongings.

9

Emmy

SHE SAT STIFFLY in the canoe, the ache in her back minuscule compared to the utter despair in her heart. Keke led them in the front as they drifted downstream, occasionally glancing backward at her as he paddled, but it was Daniel's gaze she felt searing her for most of the travel. Remnants of her tears tasted salty on her dry lips and her limbs were numb from the cold, but none of it mattered to her.

Connor was a prisoner. And she was supposed to just carry on?

With the way Daniel reacted when she tried to refuse him, she was certain that he was more entwined in her future than he was letting on. Although she read the regret in his eyes as surely as she could see the steadfast resolve on his face, she swore there was more to his words when the flicker of something deeper flashed between them. *Why did he think he had the power to control her, or to keep her from going anywhere?* Was it due to his seventeenth-century sense of honor? Or was it stubborn arrogance that drove him because they shared intimacy, that suddenly he regarded her as under his command? She knew how men operated in the time, and she was aware that women were, for the most part, subservient and submissive, but a nagging whisper told her that there was much more to his behavior than simple male pride.

She told herself that none of it mattered, that Daniel was the fool. She was stronger than that, and she could not allow a moment of pleasure to change her course – not when it meant abandoning her brother or failing in her duty to get to Smithfield. If he thought he had the right to control her because they nearly slept together, he had another thing coming.

Oh, yes. Daniel was keeping something from her – and she was going to figure out exactly what that was.

They made quick time in daylight and did not stop until after dusk had fallen. It took a fair amount of time to navigate through the narrow waterways tangled through the upper falls area, and they had not covered much distance until the river widened near Bermuda Hundred. By nightfall she gauged that they had traveled nearly twenty miles down the James River, but she was not certain of her judgment and she knew she had missed many landmarks as frustration clouded her thoughts.

Ahi Kekeleksu was a curious fellow. Daniel called him Keke, which seemed an odd nickname for such a ferocious looking man. He stood about the same height as Daniel but his body filled out with solid brawn, his legs and arms thick with muscles wrought like those of a fighter. His hair was a dark ebony shade and he wore it long, with a single grey tipped feather twined near his ear. Like Daniel, he wore a mixed assortment of clothes which were neither English or native, rough homespun brown breeches and a loose tunic, topped with a bearskin cloak trimmed in rabbit fur along the edges of his face. Beneath his cloak she could see the handle of a sword on his back; it was held securely by a leather harness that crisscrossed his chest and back. It seemed an oddity for a native man to wear, but considering that they were men who lived in two worlds, perhaps it made sense.

Once darkness shielded them, Keke and Daniel pulled the canoe up onto a quiet spot on the riverbank. Daniel muttered something about sweeping the area and left her with Keke, so she lowered her heavy pack to the sand and sat down.

"Here," Keke said, dropping a hand ax at her feet. "Dig. We need a fire."

She stared mutely at him, her temper rising. *Just who the hell did he think he was, ordering her around?* She bit back a harsh retort and reminded herself of what time she was in. It was normal behavior for a man, and it would do her no good to fight him.

He grunted his approval when she snatched the ax and started to dig. He brought a pile of driftwood to her and lined the Firehole with dry sand grass, and she watched as he tied a length of twine to a stick to make a bow drill. While he worked on his task, she rummaged through her backpack and found her fire steel. She struck it with a scraper and a flash of spark fell onto the kindling, lighting up with an audible *whoosh* and startling Keke, who stared curiously at her.

"What kind of fire stick is that?" he asked.

She held it up, shrugging. "It's a fire steel. It's made from carbon, it lights up fast."

He took it from her hands to peer at it, then handed it back to her, seemingly not impressed. *He certainly was a cocky son of a gun,* she mused.

"What time are you from?" he asked. He kept his eyes on the fire, feeding the flame by pushing logs into it with a long stick. She was taken slightly aback by his question, but quickly recovered.

"Two thousand fourteen," she said quietly.

He whistled low in response, shaking his head. "'Tis a long time away. Did the travel pain you, when you came through?"

She nodded. "Yes. It was awful. Like being torn apart, except you're being squeezed, all at once. I don't know how else to describe it."

"The others speak little of it. I often wondered how it felt, to travel such a way," he replied.

She pulled her knees to her chest and rested her chin on her crossed arms, letting the warmth of the flickering amber flames licks at the coldness in her bones. "I never wanted this," she said softly, more to herself than to him. "I never wanted to come here. I never wanted any of this."

"Hmpf," he said, tossing bark onto the fire. "You are where you belong, have no doubt of that. Your kind always returns home."

"This isn't my home," she answered.

"It is," he said, a simple statement of fact rather than an argument. "And soon you will see your path."

Daniel returned. He spoke to Keke in their native tongue, and it pricked at her pride that he chose to communicate that way when he knew she did not understand their language. The men spoke in rapid succession, and she was frustrated that she knew nothing of what they discussed.

She got up and walked away from them, following the edge of the water. Pulling the Bloodstone out from beneath the folds of her dress, she wrapped her fingers around it and felt comforted by the familiar warmth. *Was she truly where she was supposed to be, or had the power taken her astray?* Why send her brother to the past with her, only to take him away when she needed him most? It was easy to believe that some grave error occurred with the magic, but the reality of ending up with Daniel and knowing who he was, surely was too much coincidence.

Frustrated tears sprang to her eyes at the thought of Connor and she angrily wiped them away with her closed fist. She heard him come up behind her, his feet on the sand making soft swishing sounds as he walked.

"Leave me alone," she said. "I'm not going back there."

Daniel placed his hand on her shoulder and pulled her to face him. She shrugged off his hand but turned, fighting off her weakness, putting a hard mask across her face rather than display how she felt utterly confused by the events of the day.

"What are you doing?" he asked, his eyes fixed on the Bloodstone in her hand. She dropped it, shaking her head.

"I can't go with you, Daniel. You don't understand. My entire life was planned for this moment, and I cannot just abandon it. Why do you insist I must go with you?"

"Because you will run to those who will harm you. You think the Ricahecrians will treat you kindly? You think they will welcome you and release your brother on your simple request?" he replied, his words biting painfully at her resolve. His hands tightened on her shoulders, and a part of her longed to pretend there was no discord between them, if only for a moment.

"I don't know. I just know he wouldn't abandon me if I was captured," she said quietly. "And if I can't do anything for him, then I have to go on. I have to make it to Smithfield, or all of this has been for nothing."

It was the truth she was bound to honor. Surely, a man like Daniel could understand that. What words she thought might resonate with him failed miserably, seeming to inflame him even more. His usually kind face darkened, his jaw tightening and his lips twisted into a scowl.

She suddenly felt a pressure and a sharp tug at her neck. The lanyard holding her Bloodstone snapped from the pressure of Daniel's hand. She gasped as he pulled it away from her and deposited it in the fold of his cloak.

"Give it back to me!" she shouted, immediately going on the defensive. He easily deflected her blows, pushing her seeking hands away until she landed a solid slap to his cheek, which seemed to stun him long enough for her to grab her gun.

She leveled it at him, her hands shaking so hard she could not focus on the sight. Nor could she pull the trigger, and she was certain that he knew it as well.

"Give. Me. My. Bloodstone," she demanded. *How dare he?* One moment he held her tenderly as if her voice and thoughts mattered, yet all along he had planned to take her stone?

"Enough!" he roared. He snatched her wrists and the gun went off, sending one of her precious bullets into the trees. He disarmed her in the blink of a moment when she hesitated, thrusting her arms behind her hard enough to bring tears to her eyes once more. She cried out in a mixture of fury and frustration and brought her heel down hard on his foot, throwing him off balance long enough for her to twist away from his grasp and run.

She sprinted across the sand, but she was in no position to get very far with the heavy skirt bunching up between her knees. Before she could even think about what she was doing or where she was running to, he caught her by one arm and twisted her around, sending them both to the ground. She tried to scramble away from him but he grabbed her fists and slammed them to the sand, the weight of his body imprisoning her.

"Do you think I will let you run to your death?" he shouted, his face close to hers. "Do you think so little of me? Your brother is lost. They *know* he is a Time Walker. They used his blood and bled him dry to heal their sick people. If you go to the Ricahecrians, you will die. If you go alone to the place you call Smithfield, you will die!"

He was no longer her gentle Daniel. A stranger replaced the man she had given her heart to, one she did not recognize as he stared down at her. He was a beast of an unrestrained man with rage flaring through him, barely contained beneath his obsidian eyes and cold countenance. He fumbled with her wrists and she gasped when she realized he bound them together with a length of twine that cut into her flesh.

"Am I your prisoner now?" she whispered.

"You saved my life, and I will save yours now – even when you seek certain death," he muttered. He sat up and tucked her gun into his belt beneath the shelter of his cloak. Her eyes followed the motion, and she

125

realized that getting either the gun or the Bloodstone back from him was going to be impossible while he still breathed air.

When she refused to move he grabbed her by the chin. She stared insolently back at him.

"Walk, or I will drag you," he said.

"Don't touch me. Don't ever touch me again," she replied. She jerked away and struggled to her feet, which was a difficult task without the full use of her hands. She walked back towards camp of her own accord, twisting her wrists against her bonds while she plotted how she was going to get herself out of the mess she was in.

DANIEL LEFT TO patrol the area while they had a few hours to sleep, leaving her in the company of his cousin in the dark of night. Keke rested on his back, his arms crossed over his chest, occasionally raising one eyelid a bit to peer at her.

"I need to eat something," she finally said. She could not sleep and she desperately regretted leaving the turkey meat stashed in the snow bank at the cottage. Her stubborn streak demanded that she would be damned if she'd let either one of her captors get a good night's rest while she was sitting there bound and miserable.

She sat up onto her knees, pulling her cloak close around her neck with the tips of her cramped fingers. A cold breeze drifted off the river, sending a chill down her spine and a rash of goosebumps over her skin. The fire was banked and low, only a muted glow beneath the light of the moon that illuminated the sand around them.

"Do not think of running," Keke warned with a long sigh. "I will catch you, and I am not as kind as my cousin."

Emmy bristled at the threat, but at the same time, she believed him. Despite the change in Daniel, she had some evidence of his more reasonable side. With Keke, however, it was a different story. If ever there was a notion in her head of what a dangerous warrior might be, it was him, sitting across from her with a sick sense of humor and an increasingly small tolerance for her resistance.

"I need to pee," she insisted.

"Do you always talk so much?" Keke muttered.

"I'm not making idle conversation. I really have to go," she shot back. She pushed her bound hands into the sand and managed to struggle to her feet, getting caught in the heavy layers of her dress and nearly tripping over onto her head in the process.

Keke groaned his displeasure and followed her to the edge of the wood line, turning his back obligingly while she squatted. While he gave her a few moments of privacy, she searched the ground until she found a rock with a jagged edge.

"Be quick," Keke demanded. She rubbed her binding on the rock, her eyes darting back and forth between her task and Keke's back. The rock was not very sharp, but it had enough of an edge that it began to fray the rope

"Almost done," she said sweetly.

She was nearly sawed through when he yanked her to her feet.

"My cousin says you are smart, but I think not so much," Keke said. She let the insult go unmatched, losing the willpower to fight when he re-tied her wrists.

"I don't want to go with you," she said, trying to reason with him. "You must be tired of babysitting me. Wouldn't you rather sleep? Just let me go. Tell him I escaped."

He let out a chuckle, shaking his head, as if the very thought of helping her completely baffled him.

"You know nothing of loyalty if you think I would do that," he replied. He tightened the knot on her wrists with a firm yank, his brows darting downward over his dark eyes. "And you know nothing of Daniel if you think he will ever let you go."

"He doesn't own me. He has no right to make me stay."

"Hmpf," Keke replied. Stepping back, he dropped her wrists. "Daniel was only a boy when he read that book. Do you know what it does to a man, to know his fate? To know how he will meet his end, and when it will happen? When you look on the day of your birth, and you count the days of your life, your count grows. When Daniel counts, he counts the days he has left," Keke said quietly. "Perhaps he has no right, as you say, but he will do what he must to keep you. He knows that time is short, and he will not waste it."

Emmy stared back at him, wordless. *What a terrible burden to bear. Yet could Daniel expect her to abandon her path, when he was so dedicated to following his own? And why did she still feel something for him, when he had bound her like a dog and forced her to stay?*

"If not for him, I would leave you. I would let you run to the Ricahecrians and let them drain you dry. Be glad of the loyalty I have for my cousin. Be glad it is not me who decides what to do with you," he said. It was not menace in his tone, but pure truth, sending a sickening feeling into the pit of her empty stomach.

She let him take her back to camp without resistance, resuming her spot by the fire. She closed her eyes to reality, and tried to lose herself in the blessed darkness of sleep.

10

Daniel

"SO, COUSIN," KEKE said, shoving his shoulder into Daniel as they walked, "Will you mend things with her, or will you keep her tied? I fear she will stab us while we sleep if we release her, but dragging her along until we arrive at the Pamunkey village will delay our travel for sure."

Daniel sighed. He was aware that Keke attempted to counter his foul mood, as his cousin was a man always ready with a teasing jibe in the face of adversity, but Daniel had too much on his mind to accept the camaraderie of shared humor.

"I took her Bloodstone and her weapon. She mourns her loss and her thoughts are confused. I am afraid she will run – or worse, use the stone," Daniel replied. "She is strong, and stubborn, and fierce. She will not listen to reason." The sand was packed firm where they walked along the riverbank. Although cold enough for need of layers and his heavy cloak, the air was clear and the rays from the rising amber sun felt warm over the calm water. If the Ricahecrians tracked them by land, then Daniel and the others would have time to reach the

Pamunkey village. If their enemies came by water, it was a different matter.

Daniel glanced back at Emmy, who was still sleeping by the remnants of the doused fire. Her bound hands were tucked up beneath her chin, curled into the folds of her cloak. Even at a distance, he could see the remnants of dusty tear trails on her cheeks, and he could see the weariness in the lines of her sweet face. It pained him to cause her distress, but the thought of what would happen to her if she went to the Ricahecrians shadowed all regret. If it meant she hated him, then so be it. He would save her from herself.

"Ah, I see. So did you think taking that from her would make her docile?" Keke asked.

"I had no choice. I saw her brother with the Ricahecrians. He was a slave to their War Chief, and they knew he was a Blooded One. It seems that other tribes still tell the tale of what power the Blooded Ones bear," Daniel said. He explained what happened at the battle at the Falls, and how he had promised Wicawa Ni Tu the life of his captive's woman before the English betrayed them all.

"And so you have promised her to our enemy," Keke concluded.

"I thought I promised the life of a stranger. Even then, it was not a choice I wished to make, but if it meant peace, then I was prepared to give it. Wicawa Ni Tu wants a Time Walker so he can heal his sick people. He says many have fallen ill with fever and they suffer greatly."

Keke looked curiously at him, shaking his head.

"You know how the magic works. Only the blood of an infant can heal many. If you gave them your woman, it would take all of her blood, all of her life force, to heal just one dying man."

"I know," Daniel agreed. He knew exactly how the magic worked, and he knew it well when he made the pact with Wicawa Ni Tu. At the time, none of it was truly real to him, nor did he care about the life of a person he did not yet know. Standing next to his cousin and looking at the sleeping woman that he loved, however, it was a different matter, one that tore at his insides in a way he might never forgive himself for.

"I saw you go into the water after the battle. I thought you were dead," Keke confessed. Daniel was somewhat surprised to see the flare of anguish on his cousin's face. Keke was a man who looked hard on first appearance, but beneath his stony exterior was the heart of a loyal man who loved his kin, and Daniel was grateful to stand beside him.

"Yet you still searched for me," Daniel countered.

"Yes. Even if it was only to return your body to our uncle, I would find you. Idiot," Keke replied, adding the insult for good measure. "Lucky for you that I arrived when I did. I fear you were about to be deflowered."

Memories of the moment Keke arrived flashed through his head. Daniel felt the heat rise to his throat. The image of Emmy lying there with her shift spread open, naked for him, with her hair streaming out like a honey colored banner across the pillow, sent an ache straight to his core that reminded him of all he had to lose.

"Ah, enough, *lucht*," Daniel growled, shooting back at him half-heartedly with a Norse insult to his manhood that they both knew well.

He helped Keke pull the canoe out to the water, and Keke finished packing their meager supplies while Daniel went to wake Emmy.

By the tears of the Gods, yes, she angered him. For what they had known of each other, and what they had shared, how could she look at him with eyes of mistrust? He hated to see the darkness of fear in her face, yet still, it burned him when she refused to listen to reason. Was it a product of the time she was born to, or was it from the teachings she endured? From the little she told him of her life, she had been raised for the purpose of fulfilling a duty – and he knew in his heart what a heavy burden such a thing was to carry.

"Emmy," he said, kneeling down beside her. He ran his hand over her hair next to her ear, trying to rouse her gently from her sleep. She squirmed and opened her eyes, immediately looking up to meet his gaze. At once, she shifted and sat up, pulling away from his touch, and although he did not wish to be coarse with her, it fueled his frustration even more.

"Don't touch me!" she hissed. He muttered a curse in a language she did not understand and snatched her bound hands to him, slicing through the thin rope with his knife before she could fight him any further. Keke was right. He could not keep her bound as they traveled, they needed her cooperation if they were to travel with any speed.

"We do not know if the Ricahecrians are tracking us, or if they follow us by land, or by water. They could be hours behind or a day behind. If we leave now, we may arrive at the Pamunkey village by nightfall, and then you can rage at me all you like," he said, leaving no edge of softness in his voice. "Until then, do as you are told, or I will bind you again."

She rubbed at her wrists and he narrowed his eyes when he saw the raw red marks on her skin. It was for his actions that she was pained, but what other choice did he have? He could only hope that the few hours of sleep had softened her, or at least given her the recovery she needed in order to carry on.

"How much farther to the village?" she asked, her voice unwavering at she stared at him. She gave no hint of submission, choosing to carefully avoid agreement with his terms. If he was not so preoccupied with keeping her safe, he might have admired the show of strength, yet with the situation being what it was, her response only served to irritate him more.

"A day's travel at best. At worst, we will camp tonight downstream and reach the Pamunkey in the morning," he replied. He turned away from her but was stopped by another request.

"I want my gun returned to me. And my Bloodstone," she said. He paused, shifting slightly so that he could see her standing behind him. With her fingers clenched in fists at her side and her cheeks flushed bright pink, she was every bit the flaming banshee he once thought might deliver him to the afterworld. Stray damp ringlets of her honeyed hair stuck to the sides of her face, curling to outline her heart shaped face and bright green eyes.

Despite her bluster, despite her defiance, he wanted much more from her, and even as she made demands of him, he wished to mend the damage between them.

"You are safe now, so why must you carry it?" he asked.

Her scowl leveled into a thin line, and the hint of something dark shimmered in her gaze.

"It's all I have to protect myself," she said quietly. "It came from my time. I never wanted to travel to the past. I never wanted to have this duty. I'm doing it for my brother – and for my mother. And having it reminds me of what I am, and what I am supposed to do. It ties me to them so I won't forget."

Daniel considered her confession, her words tearing at him worse than the wound from a blade ever could. He knew what she would someday be to him, and it was that truth that he held onto when he answered her.

"I will protect you, *eholen*, have no doubt," he said. "And you need no weapon to remember those you love."

He left her then and resumed packing, feeling as if he left a part of his heart with her when he went.

THEY TRAVELED MOST of the day, the strong downstream current carrying them quickly towards their destination. Although they passed a Weanock village where he had friends, Daniel did not want to lose any time by stopping, but by the time the sun settled down beneath the glimmer of the river and dusk fell upon them, they had to stop for the night.

"Does this spot suit you, Miss Cameron?" Keke asked, his words tinged with a hint of sarcasm. Daniel did not miss the intent, and he grunted a coarse reply in their Paspahegh language so that Emmy would not understand.

"Leave her be," Daniel warned his cousin. "If you taunt her, it will not end well for any of us."

"Hmpf. She is just a woman. What harm could she be to me?" Keke replied. They guided the boat up onto the river's edge and they both jumped into the shallow water to pull it further in.

"She is much stronger than she looks. She dragged me from the river to her cottage with only her two hands. I have no doubt she could be much trouble, if she set her mind to it."

"If she has been no trouble until now, as you say, then I fear what trouble she will be with *trying*," Keke grumbled. "I know I shall sleep with one eye open tonight, if I sleep at all."

Daniel grinned and slapped his cousin on the back. He left Keke to secure the boat behind a low wall of boulders and moved to assist Emmy onto the sand, but she was well ahead of him and jumped out on her own, clearing the water with enough distance to keep her boots from getting wet.

He could not help studying her for a moment, his throat dry and tight as he took her in. She wore her satchel over one shoulder and she absently rubbed one of her wrists, her eyes searching their landing spot with a cautious glare. He was loathed to admit how much it bothered him that she ignored him, or that he had to step into her immediate space to elicit an acknowledgment.

"There's a small cave up there above the flat rocks. It should be suitable for us to shelter in for a few hours," he said, keeping his voice level as if there was only casual conversation between them. She shrugged, barely glancing at him.

"I suppose it will do. We have no other choice right now if we want to rest and eat," she said.

"Keke has some dried meat in his pack. It is enough to sate our bellies for now."

"I still have a full flask of cider, too," she murmured.

He walked with her to the mouth of the shallow cave. It was partially recessed into the side of a hill, with large flat rocks forming a slight overhang at the entrance. Emmy fumbled in her satchel and produced a long, round object that lit up like a torch when she pressed on the end, illuminating the entire cave and saving Daniel the trouble of making a fire right away.

"It's a flashlight," she quickly explained when he raised a questioning brow. She handed the object to him and Daniel was surprised to feel the entire thing was warm in his palm. "It's like a torch, but without fire. See the soft button on the end? If you push on that, it turns on and off."

He did as she instructed, fascinated when the torch blinked off. He hit the button a few times, testing it, letting the light hit beneath his chin at first, then rotating it so that it created a halo of light on the roof of the cave above their heads. Emmy moved closer then, and when he turned it off once more and thrust them into darkness, he felt her fist grip him and twist into a knot on the front of his tunic.

"Ok, turn it back on," she said. *"Please."* He noted the edge of panic in her words and immediately did as she asked, holding the flashlight in his lowered hand so that the light illuminated them from below. He felt her tremble and suddenly recalled how she always slept with a candle or fire burning, so he pressed the light into her hand.

"Tell me," he said, placing his hand gently over hers where she still clutched his tunic. "Why do you fear the darkness?"

Her throat tightened and the tiny lines at the edges of her eyes deepened as she looked up at him in the white glow of the light.

"I don't – not really," she replied. "I mean, maybe I do. I've had nightmares since I was a child, so it's just an old habit. I just don't like being trapped in dark places."

"You are not trapped now," he said softly.

"Am I not?" she replied, tearing a hole in his heart with her bitter response. He slipped his hand into her hair, caressing her cheek lightly with his thumb as he met her stare.

"No. I stand here in the darkness with you. I will never let you face it alone," he whispered. With all that had happened between them he knew it was a risk, but he drew her close and held her in his arms, feeling the racing beat of her heart against his chest.

When her tense arms relaxed and she let out a long, slow breath, he brushed his lips against the side of her face and gently whispered in her ear.

"Tell me what chases the fear away," he said. She shivered but did not pull away, leaning into his embrace instead. "In your time, how did you stop it? How did you face it?"

She ducked her head, leaning her forehead against his.

"I – I listened to music," she replied. "On my iPod. It's a thing that plays music. I didn't tell Connor that I brought it with me. He'd be angry."

"Did you bring it with you?" Daniel asked. He could not rightly picture what she was describing to him, but he was curious to learn and glad to know there was a way to ease her distress. She shifted and fumbled through her satchel, pulling out a small silver box that fit snugly in the palm of her hand. Attached to the flat box were two long white cords, each with a rounded soft grey tip that curled into a crescent shape at the ends.

"How does it work?" he asked, fascinated how the box surged to life and emitted a glow very similar to the flashlight. He recalled his aunt telling stories about some of the devices from her future time so he was not too suspicious of the box Emmy held, but to see it in front of him was a different matter.

"Here, be still," she said. She took one of the curved pieces and gently tucked it into his ear, causing him a moment of apprehension as it muffled his hearing. "Don't be alarmed. Just listen."

She pressed her finger on the light and suddenly he heard the easy rhythm of a song. It sounded like the music he once heard at the English Governor's home when he accompanied his uncle on a visit there as a child. He recalled they made the music not with drums or their voices, but with instruments that they used to produce the sound, and that the players all read from pieces of paper so they could play in unison.

The sound in his ear was low at first and gradually increased, causing him to draw sharply back, but she placed her hand on his chest and he relaxed. She placed the other curved piece in her ear and immediately her breathing seemed to slow.

"It's called Canon in D Major. My mother used to play this for me when I couldn't sleep. It sounds like sunshine and light, and it made the darkness fade away," she said. "It was written by a man named Pachelbel ... I don't know if he's even been born yet."

He could see why she compared the music to the sun, as there was no other way to describe the beauty of the sound in his ear. When he felt her sway with the gentle rhythm of the music he joined her, and between them the flashlight fell to the ground, rolling a few feet away and spilling a halo of light at their feet. She tensed for a moment and tried to pull away at the flash of light but he would not let her go, holding her tight and moving with her to the pace of the song.

"Do not look at the darkness," he said when her gaze dipped downward. He pressed his lips to her ear, taking in the sweet scent of her, and he whispered words of comfort to her that he knew she did not understand. "*Kacha wishasihan, eholen*," he murmured. *You are safe now, my beloved.*

She did not flinch when the blaze of the flashlight dimmed and began to fade, as if she expected it to happen, and he continued to speak softly in her ear as they held each other. They held their heads close and danced, letting the song take them to a place where she was safe, and where he could shelter her from the cold darkness of the world if only he could keep her in his arms.

Let me be your light, he thought, looking down at her while the glow of the flashlight flickered and went out. The song ended and they stopped dancing, the sound of their breathing the only echo of sound in the hollowness of the cave. Before she could flee he took her face in his hands and kissed her, not knowing if it was the right thing to do but wanting to do it all the same.

Her fists tightened on his tunic and she kissed him back, and in the sparse light of the moon that filtered into the cave he could see the glow of her face and taste the wetness of salty tears on her mouth. He traced his lips over her cheeks, kissing the tears away as he whispered soothing words in her ear, and she held onto him as if she believed them.

"See?" he whispered. "There is no darkness here." In all his days he had never known what it was to shelter another, to have someone he wished to keep from all harm. He once viewed his life as expendable because he knew the day of his death, yet with her in his arms she was all he could think of, and he knew that he would deny his god and his purpose and even his own life if it meant she would rest easy when the moon rose high overhead each night.

Daniel heard the snap and crackle and smelled the scent of charred cypress bark before he saw the flame Keke carried. He reluctantly let Emmy go when she stepped back and the curved piece fell from his ear, noting that she scooped up her flashlight and shoved it into the belt at her waist.

"There is wood nearby for a fire, cousin," Keke said, his eyes shifting to Emmy, who was shoving her music device into her satchel. He raised a curious brow and Daniel scowled. He was in no mood for his cousin's taunts, so he interrupted any humorous jibes his cousin wished to make and took the torch from Keke's hand.

"Good. Leave this here and help me fetch it," he said curtly. He held the torch out to Emmy, who took it from him without question. He could see the rapid rise and fall of her breasts and the way her cheeks flushed crimson pink and he did not wish to leave her. Yet she needed the warmth of a fire and a few hours of rest just as much as he did.

"Stay here and I will return," he said, meeting her gaze. "We will not be long."

"I'm fine," she replied. Her voice rang steady, her eyes now dry, and if the stubborn twist of her downturned mouth was meant to convince him then it surely served the purpose. He had known her only a short time but he felt as if he knew her soul, and by that certainty he knew she was made of something stronger. She had her moment of weakness and pushed it aside, and now she was through with any thoughts of self-pity.

And he loved her for it.

11

Emmy

SHE TOSSED HER backpack over one shoulder and walked off to find a spot to relieve herself. After she found a suitable space a few yards away which was private yet still illuminated somewhat by the firelight of the torch she jammed into a pile of rocks, she squatted and did her business despite the ridiculous trappings of the dress she wore. She rifled through her pack in search of the travel tissues she knew she'd stuffed inside, regretting using one but feeling in no mood to look for suitable leaves in the dark.

When she replaced the bundle of travel tissues, her fingers scraped over the rough edge of the book. It was the *Leabhar Sinnsreadh,* The Book of the Blooded Ones, and she had promised her brother that she would not read what it contained.

She pulled it out and leaned back against a tree, twisting the end off her flashlight to slip two new batteries inside. It was all she had left and she didn't particularly know what to do with the old batteries, so she quickly made a small shallow hole in the ground with the heel of her boot and buried them.

Emmy squinted at the book, shining her flashlight on the blasted thing. Yes, it was just as she recalled – not that she ever paid it much attention. Considering what it meant to her now, it was strange that she had gone most of her life and had never wished to read it. Although she had ready access to it, she'd always done what she was told to do; she obeyed her brother's orders without question. Yet with Connor's death and her world thrust into chaos, everything had changed. *Was there some mistake? Was she in the wrong time? The answers must be inside.* Perhaps the pull she felt for Daniel was nothing more than age old lust, and their meeting was nothing more than chance. After all, how could she care for a man who thought nothing of tying her up to bend her to his will?

As old as the book was, it was still solid bound. The thick cover was weathered but intact, made from what she imagined was tree bark and stretched leathered animal skin for the cover, which she tentatively opened.

"You know that book is not meant for your eyes," Daniel said. His presence startled her, causing her to slam the book shut and grip it to her chest.

"It's my right to know," she replied, turning on him with the edge of despair fueling her thoughts. "My brother is gone. I'm alone in this world, and I need to know *why* I'm here. Don't I deserve that much, after everything I gave up? Leaving my home – my brother's life?"

"And you will know why, when the time is right. There can be no good of knowing these things before they happen. There is a reason that book is held by those who will guard it; there is a reason why the living should not know their fate," he answered.

144

She backed up when he came closer, wincing when she felt the bark of a tree against her spine. His eyes darkened at her motion but she stared defiantly at him in return, daring him to demand anything more of her. She chastised herself for nearly giving everything to him, her mind swimming at the implications of what had happened between them since the day she saved his life. She wanted to trust him – more than anything she had ever wanted in her life – yet the notion that he was holding something back from her was a flash of warning racing through her head like a blinking orange neon sign.

"Tell me the truth. Tell me everything you know – what you read in this book – and I won't look. But if you won't tell me the truth, it's my only choice," she demanded. "Tell me why you're holding my Bloodstone. Why does it matter to you if I leave?"

He reached out and rested one hand next to her shoulder, closing the space between them. The glow of the moon washed over them when a break in the clouds appeared overhead, illuminating the way his eyes softened and the lines of his face eased as he looked at her. She swallowed hard, biting back the urge to let him comfort her, when she could clearly see he wanted to do it.

She could not succumb to letting him comfort her, when all it did was serve to smother her good sense.

"Give me your word that you will not read it, and I will tell you what you seek," he said. She nodded, frozen in place, her eyes locked onto his.

"Yes. I promise," she agreed. He sighed.

"You are meant to be here – right here, beside me in this place. You will have a journey, but it will not be to

145

the place you seek. I will accompany you, and I know it to be true."

She gripped the book harder. His eyes bore through her as if he were searching into her soul.

"Why will you go with me?" she asked, knowing the answer in her heart but needing to hear it from his lips.

"Because I will end my days at your side," he said softly. "Because you will be my wife, and you will someday bear my sons." She felt the rush of hot tears and did nothing to stop them, letting the truth echo in her heart as she looked at him.

His wife. His sons.

Of course. How could she have ever doubted it was anything else? The pull she felt for him, the bond between them – it was like instinct, as if she had no choice in the matter. And suddenly she knew she never would.

"Then why don't you want me to read it?" she asked, her voice barely above a whisper.

He lowered his head, his cheek next to hers so that the warmth of his breath fell onto her skin and stirred her to her core.

"Because once you read it, you will not stop at knowing your future," he said. "You will keep reading until you find your end, and that is a burden that I do not want you to carry."

"You know – you know when it will happen?" she asked, her words trailing off. He knew what she meant, and he nodded.

"Yes. I know when my time ends, and I know how it will happen. I know when we will part, and I tell you this: it is a story no man should know. When I first read it, I denied that it was real, yet now, here you are, standing before me, and I have held you in my arms. And I know now that this is my destiny, that my path is tangled with yours." He pressed his lips gently to her ear and she softened in his arms, leaning against him to keep the entire world from spinning.

"I'm sorry," she whispered.

He shook his head. "I am not, nor will I ever be. You are mine, have no doubt."

Daniel pressed something into her hand, and she immediately felt the warmth of her Bloodstone. Once she closed her fingers over it, he tucked her gun into her belt and stepped away from her.

"We all still have a choice, no matter what has been written. I choose to follow our destiny; I choose you. If you must leave this time and forever leave my side, then take my life with your weapon. Stop the beating of my heart and end this ache in my blood for you," he said.

He turned away and left her there. She watched him go, feeling as if part of her lifeblood drained as he went.

SHE REMAINED AT the edge of the riverbank until the gleam of the moon was clear in the night sky and the stars glimmered like beacons of shame above her head. *How did she know he was telling the truth, if she did not read the book herself?* With all that had happened between them, the very notion of mistrust was a weight deep in her bones. If she had to wager her faith in Daniel over what she had been raised to believe, then at that moment she knew with all her soul that she would choose him. After looking into his eyes and feeling the warmth of his steady hands upon her skin, there was only the truth that mattered.

If Daniel meant her harm, he could have taken her life at any time. Yes, he had taken her Bloodstone and her gun, and yes, he had bound her hands and forced her to obey him. Yet he did not need to stay with her once his wounds healed, nor did he need to save her by killing the Ricahecrian scout. He did not need to hold her in his arms or promise to help her on her path. Beyond what tender feelings she imagined between them, there was that indisputable truth. Daniel did not seem the sort of man to taunt his prey; if his intentions were not pure, she would be dead by now. And if she believed his words, then his role in her life was much more complicated than simple chance.

"Because I will end my days at your side," he said softly. "Because you will be my wife, and you will someday bear my sons."

His wife. His sons.

It was beyond what she had ever thought might happen. Of course, she considered that she might eventually be married and live out some semblance of a normal life in the seventeenth century. All of her life she had been told to protect her secret and that she must complete her task in the past over all else. Yet once that was finished, was it possibly true that she would live as a wife to Daniel?

The woman she once was in the future seemed a distant memory to what she had become. She was once taught to see through the mask of men who would try to control her, to use her for their own twisted means. With her mother long dead and Connor gone, there was no one to tell her she was a fool or that she was simply blinded by the strength of her feelings for Daniel.

"If you must leave this time and forever leave my side, then take my life with your weapon. Stop the beating of my heart and end this ache in my blood for you," he said.

She recalled the way his eyes bore into hers with his declaration and the way a flush of heat roved over her skin at his words. Emmy had no explanation for the steady faith in Daniel's heart, nor did she know what she had done to earn such devotion – until he confessed the truth. His stalwart purpose should make her feel comforted, but instead she was broken by his strength.

The weight of the gun tucked in her belt tugged her long skirt down. There was one lone bullet left, a single shot at holding onto that life she left behind in the future. Her attachment to the firearm seemed such an odd thing, yet still, it was a symbol of the time she was born to and she was not yet ready to lose that last piece of herself. As long as she had it, she could hold onto some semblance of independence, as if she retained some control over her tenuous destiny in the seventeenth century.

"I'm sorry, Momma," Emmy said. *Perhaps it was time to trust Daniel in every way. Perhaps she was truly meant to follow his guidance.* The darkness did not answer and her words trailed off as a whisper in the night. There was so much she wanted to say, if only her mother was there to hear it.

Instead, she gathered her courage and made her way up the slope of the riverbank. Under the shallow overhang of the flat rocks she could see the glow of the fire. As she approached, a shadow moved and her breath stuck in her throat until she realized it was only Keke. His stoic face held quiet reserve when he surveyed her, and he issued a chuckle when she reached his side.

"Have you returned for more fighting?" he asked, the edge of his lip curled up.

"I don't want to fight," she replied. He made a low grunt.

"Hmpf. Maybe so. I hope you both are not bleeding when I return. I think my cousin is a fool for putting a weapon in your hand."

"I would never hurt him like that," she shot back.

"Maybe not with your gun," he said. "But there are other ways to hurt a man. It takes only your words to draw blood."

It was her turn to scoff then. "He's stronger than that."

Keke reached out and took hold of the Bloodstone pendant hanging from her neck. He held it for a moment, staring at the dark stone, and then his gaze shifted upwards to meet hers.

"Yes, he is strong," he said. "Yet you? You will always make him bleed."

She swallowed down against her dry throat. He dropped the pendant and turned away from her before she could respond, his leather-clad feet crunching on the loose gravel path along the riverbank as he left to patrol.

The amber flicker of firelight in the warm alcove drew her back to Daniel. He was sprawled out near the fire, his arms crossed behind his head as a makeshift pillow. His torso was bereft of his tunic, bared and dark skinned and utterly distracting, and she could see that he had removed his bandage as well. The wound puckered his flesh, healed into a dark red line with the tips of her stitching sticking out at one end. For a moment she was caught in the simple beauty of him, entranced by the man who had given so freely of himself to see her safe. If there was such a thing as a hero, he was hers, a snippet of fantasy alive and real before her eyes.

Daniel sat up when he saw her. She kneeled down beside him, her breath hitching when his warm hand slid over her knee.

"I don't know where I am meant to be," she said. "I don't know what I'm meant to do." Taking the gun from her belt, she placed it down carefully next to the fire. His eyes followed the gun and she held her breath until his gaze shifted back to hers.

She thought she should tell him she was sorry, that the harsh words she spoke were remnants of her long-held fears, yet as he looked at her she realized he already knew. Relinquishing the gun was her unspoken surrender to him, to all that he had become to her and all that he might be in her future. He acknowledged the gesture with a slight nod and she knew that he understood what it cost her.

He slipped his fingers into her hair and drew her close, his eyes latched onto hers.

"Right now, in this time, you are meant to be here," he said, his words hoarse but steady. He kissed her, clutching his hand gently in her hair as his lips roamed over hers. It was what she had been missing in the days they had battled one another. With each caress he pulled her down, mending that aching chasm between them.

When his fingers sought her dress binding, she eagerly helped him, shedding her clothes and tearing at what remained of his. His hands were everywhere, molding her flesh, holding her tight as he explored her body as if he meant to consume her. She cried out as his mouth traced over her breast, settling on her peaked nipple while he gripped her bottom with one strong hand. As much as she needed independence, she needed his control even more, and as he laid her down and stretched over her with the gleam of firelight in his dark eyes, she welcomed the possession in his touch.

"What you are meant to do is this," he murmured, his hand gripping her hip as he slid home. There was no hesitation in the motion, no pause, the swift claiming causing her to cry out. It pained her more than she thought it would. Her fingers dug into his shoulders, slipping on his slick skin and bringing a strangled groan from his lips. He pulled one of her hands up to rest above her head, pinning it down while he moved inside her.

The darkness ebbed away with each thrust, bringing her deeper down to that place where only he could touch her soul. Nothing could reach her there, except for the burn of his lips on her skin and the heat of his desire as they sought release.

"And when you are meant to go," he said, "I will go with you."

He made his promise. She abandoned her fears and gave him all that she had, and for that moment in time, it was enough.

They slept little in the few stolen hours before dawn, drifting between the rawness in their joining and the desire to taste more. Although the act was new to her and she was eager to please him, throughout the night Daniel shocked her with the way he made her body sing, sending a hum through her bones as if he plucked a finely tuned string. He was patient yet persistent in their lovemaking, leaving the mark of possession on her skin just as surely as he left it imprinted in her blood.

Later, she rested her head on his chest, listening to the steady thud of his heart beneath her ear.

"Did you always believe this would happen?" she asked softly, more to herself than to him. She was not sure she wanted to know the answer, but before she could dismiss her question, his arms tightened around her.

"Your name was in the book," he replied. "I did not know when or how I would find you, only that it would happen."

"So it's just destiny then? It's already decided because my name is there?" she asked.

"No," he said. He pulled her upwards and she slid eagerly onto his chest to take his kiss. It was gentle and slow, a remembrance of what more they might have. He shifted, settling her snug against him. She felt him stir beneath her in readiness and she smiled.

"After the battle when I opened my eyes and found I was tied to a bed, you came to me. It was then that I knew I wanted you, before I even knew your name."

"You thought I was keeping you captive," she said softly, placing a kiss at the corner of his mouth. His breath was warm on her cheek when he spoke softly, the gentle motion tickling her skin.

"I was your captive then," he whispered. "The same as I will be for all of my days."

THE SUNRISE WAS still low in the sky when they packed the canoe. If all went as planned, they would arrive at the Pamunkey village by midday and they could finally rest easy within the protection of the tribal lands. Emmy suspected Daniel did not wish to stay long, but it would be a welcome reprieve after two days of near constant travel down the James River.

She wore her fitted blue jeans beneath her chemise that morning and fitted the whale-boned stays over it, cinching it tightly at her waist to give her more freedom of movement. She decided that she was through with the constrained trappings that women in the time endured, placing the short leather boots into her backpack and replacing them with her tall sturdy ones. Yes, she knew she had to be careful, but she also needed to be functional; if they were being followed, she did not wish to be helpless, and she was acutely aware of how she stumbled and flopped around like a fish out of water when she tried to run from Daniel. She had no intention of doing anything except standing beside him if anything happened.

Tucking her gun firmly into her belt, she felt the brush of Daniel's hand at her waist and smiled. He handed her the short bow, which he helped her place across her body along with the leather quiver, and he showed her a knife with a serrated blade.

"Here," he said, bending on one knee. She shivered as he ran his hand down her thigh, resting on her calf as he tucked the knife into her boot. "Keep that hidden. 'Tis good to have it if you need it." His palm slid upward, warming her inner thigh despite the thin fabric of her jeans. When she looked down at him, slightly breathless, his gaze betrayed a hunger that shot a surge of desire straight to her core.

"You can't possibly want more," she whispered, biting back a smile. A warmth spread through her as he grinned and she recalled their sleepless night. She darted a glance in Keke's direction, and thankfully he did not seem to notice their interaction. Daniel stood up, cupping his hand over the round of her buttock and squeezing it firmly in response.

"I do," he whispered in return. "And as soon as my cousin's eyes are not upon us, I will have you again." He released her with a smirk and a low chuckle, squeezing her once more for good measure before he turned away.

In the moment that he moved, she heard a sound split the air and then a solid *thunk*. She glanced in the direction of the noise and was stunned to see a dagger impaled in the side of the canoe in the exact spot Daniel had stood only seconds prior.

"Daniel?" she said. He was already next to her again as the words left her mouth, his knife in his hand, and Keke stood up to his knees in the water with his flintlock musket drawn. She pulled her gun from her belt and cocked it, knowing she only had one bullet left but ready to use it, her pulse throbbing madly when Daniel pushed her down into the sand behind the front of the boat and they sought cover.

"Stay down!" Daniel ordered. She thrust her shoulder into his and remained beside him, clutching her gun.

A man emerged from the trees. He was dressed in a long brown overcoat and buckskin vest, opened and flapping in the breeze as he walked towards them with his long musket pointed at them. She could see a swatch of dirty straw colored hair, his skin a fair pale color beneath his flushed cheeks.

"Oh, God," she whispered, slowly rising to her feet. Daniel swore an oath and came after her, but she would not be swayed. She went to the open side of the boat and looked at the knife, immediately recognizing the stone on the intricately carved handle before Daniel stepped between her and the man.

Was it possible?

"Release her!" the man called out. "Release the woman, or I *will* shoot!"

Keke stepped out from the shallow water to stand by Daniel's side, his musket aimed and unwavering.

"You have one shot, friend, and you cannot kill us both," Daniel replied.

Emmy could wait no longer. She pushed past Daniel and broke into a run, shoving her gun back into her belt as she reached him. She barreled into him hard, throwing her arms around her brother as if he were a ghost that would fade from her sight.

It was Connor. He was alive.

"You're okay," she cried, clutching him as he hugged her with his free arm and lifted her slightly off her feet. He was filthy and tired, and she noticed that he winced at her embrace, but he was blessedly whole and undoubtedly standing there alive.

"I'm here," he assured her, his arm wrapped around her shoulders and tangled in her hair. The musket he held was still aimed, wavering in his free hand while Daniel and Keke approached, and after wiping tears from her eyes with the back of her fist, she gently pushed the gun down.

"It's okay, they're not our enemies," she explained.

"Good," Connor replied, "Because this gun is empty, and I wasn't looking forward to fighting two men with my bare hands." His body seemed to sag, his breath leaving his body with a deep sigh, and he suddenly clutched his chest and collapsed down on one knee with a groan.

"Help me," Emmy begged, frantically trying to hold her brother. Daniel and Keke moved in, and she watched numbly as they left the open riverside and carried her unconscious brother back into the shelter of the stone alcove.

"I'M FINE," CONNOR muttered, slapping at her hands when she tried to loosen his shirt. He was filthy and smelled of something rank, but even that discomfort could not quell the pure relief in her soul at seeing him alive.

"You're far from fine. What happened to you? Jesus, you stink like you took a bath in a pile of garbage," Emmy replied. She handed him her flask and he took a long sip of the whiskey-spiked cider, shaking his head a bit as he swallowed it down.

"Last of the whiskey?" he asked.

"Seriously? The hell with the whiskey, and stop avoiding my question," Emmy shot back. "Are you wounded? Let me see."

He sighed, averting his gaze. She could see the whites of his knuckles standing out as he clutched the flask, and although he looked like hell she suspected something had happened that was even more disturbing than his physical appearance.

"I'm fine, I'm just weak from the blood loss. There's nothing for you to do about it, so quit pawing me," he said. He held up his hands, revealing that both of his wrists were bound, and she could see the stains of old dark blood that had seeped through and dried on the linen. He did not appear to be actively bleeding, so she rolled her eyes but left him alone, sitting back to listen to what he had to say.

"One of the Ricahecrians noticed my scar, and he alerted the others. Their War Chief took me prisoner. Seems they have a lot of people dying right now, a bloody flux or something, even the Chief's wife and children were ill," he said, his voice low and measured. "He thought I could heal his people. I guess it's lucky for me he didn't know how to use the magic, because when his wife died he surely would have drained every last drop of my blood."

"He – he *bled* you?" she asked.

"Yeah. He didn't know it's only the newborn blood that can heal. He kept trying … over and over. One of the elders improved for a few days, so he thought my blood was working, but he realized soon enough something was wrong. I wasn't going to give him any tips, either, so he decided he wanted my woman."

"Your woman?"

"You. He wanted you. They remembered when I brought you to the village to trade. He was told the women Time Walkers held more power than the men, so he wanted you."

Emmy rocked back on her haunches, her hands clasped in her lap. *So Daniel was right*, she thought. *If she went to the Ricahecrians, she'd be dead right now.*

"Christ," she whispered. "Why did I ever doubt him?"

"Who?"

"Daniel. I tried to go to the trade village to look for you. Daniel stopped me," she said. Memories of everything Daniel had done to keep her safe suddenly burned her. Despite the humiliation of being bound like a trapped spring hare and having her gun and Bloodstone confiscated, Daniel never wavered in his promise to keep her safe.

"Him? You can't possibly trust the natives. You know what they did to our kind. Opechancanough wiped them all out – none survived."

"He's not like that," she insisted, feeling the hairs on the back of her neck stand at attention and a rush of blood surge to her cheeks. "I'd be dead if not for him. We saved each other."

Connor let out a muffled snort, launching into a coughing fit spasm from the effort.

"He's like a wounded bear, Emmy. You think he won't hurt you, because you saved his life? Look at him, for Christ's sake," Connor said. "I've known men like him. They're all safe when they're wounded. It's when he's whole again that you'll see it – what he really is. And he's not going to be what you want him to be."

She did look at Daniel then. He stood outside with Keke, his tall body outlined by the amber glow of the setting sun. She took him in, all of him, from the confident tilt of his head to the sculpted curve of his jaw. His arms were crossed over his chest, and as she looked at him he must have felt the weight of her gaze because he turned her way. He raised one thick dark brow in question, and once she issued him a smile, he nodded and turned back to his cousin.

"No, I don't believe that. I *know* him. He'd never hurt me. I don't know how it happened, but it did – I love him. And I trust him. Above anyone else."

Connor closed his eyes for a long moment. Sweat dappled his forehead and moistened his clammy skin.

She imagined his pallor was due to the bloodletting, but without the advent of modern medicine, the only remedy to heal him would be the passage of time as the blood cells in his body regenerated. *If only she still had her vial of infant blood, she could heal him herself.*

"Don't trust anyone, Emmy. Didn't I teach you better than that?" Connor said softly, barely above a whisper.

"It's not that simple," she replied.

Nor would it ever be. A shadow fell across the alcove, and she immediately knew who it was. She left Connor to doze off and turned to Daniel, certain in the knowledge of where their future would lead.

12

Daniel

CONNOR ESCAPED THE Ricahecrians during the battle in one of their dugout canoes, but the man had not emerged unscathed. Daniel noted both of his wrists were still bound with blood-stained linen, and despite the façade the man put on for his sister, it was clear that he was not well. *Did Emmy see the strange pallor of his gray-tinged skin*, Daniel wondered, *or was she so oblivious to it because of her joy at seeing him alive?*

Emmy had reluctantly left his side and went with Keke to gather some firewood, and Daniel was left alone with the man for a short time.

"Here," Daniel said, offering Connor a flask. It was whiskey-spiked cider that Emmy kept in her satchel, and Daniel thought it might numb the man's pain.

"Thank you," Connor replied. "Emmy already gave me a few sips, but I'll take more." He sat with his back against the smooth stone wall, having roused back to consciousness by the time they carried him into the sheltered alcove.

"Where are you wounded?" Daniel asked.

Connor stared blankly at him for a long moment, his blue eyes resolute with some internal struggle. He winced and nodded, as if to himself, and he slowly opened the flap of the brown coat. Over his left shoulder was a deep crimson stain, dried to nearly black, and the thin layer of the white linen shirt stuck to the wound when he unbuttoned it and pushed it open.

"I dug out the arrowhead, but I'm not accustomed to doctoring myself," Connor said.

Daniel did not flinch at the purulent odor, but the red streaks spiraling away from the jagged puncture wound like the fingers of a web were another matter. It was not a healing wound, and Daniel had seen men die from much less.

"It must have pained you to travel," Daniel said.

"Yeah, well, I had to try to find her. It was a small canoe, it wasn't too bad to manage on my own."

Daniel doubted that very much, considering the wound he suffered. The man seemed made of iron with his staunch refusal to acknowledge the severity of his injury, but it was a stance that Daniel had to admit was admirable.

"There is a healer at the Pamunkey village who can tend you," Daniel said quietly. "We should leave as soon as you are ready."

"Is that where you were taking my sister?" Connor replied. He lifted the flask with his right hand and poured a bit of the cider over the wound, letting out a moan when the liquid hit the flesh and dripped down his chest. Sweat broke out on his face and Daniel feared he might again lose consciousness, but the man gritted his jaw and managed to blot the wound dry and return his clothes to some semblance of order.

"Yes," Daniel said.

Visibly paled, Connor cast his gaze on Daniel.

162

"You know what she is – what we both are," Connor said, a statement more than a question.

"I know what she is to me," Daniel replied. "As I suspect you do as well."

Connor closed his eyes and leaned his head back. "None of this is happening the way it should. Yeah, I know who you are – and don't think for a second I don't see how you look at my sister. But she wasn't supposed to meet you yet. Something's changed."

Daniel considered the man before him, intrigued by the simple strength of his resolve. He was a man gravely wounded, yet he refused to give up on finding his sister. He was a man worthy of respect, and it was then that Daniel knew where Emmy's confidence and strength had been cultivated.

"Changed?"

"Yeah, I'm sure of it," Connor replied. "According to the Book of the Blooded Ones, Emmy and I should have been here later, and she shouldn't have met you until she reached Smithfield. I think we've managed to screw things up pretty good."

"If what you say is true, then it must mean time itself changes what is written in the book. The book here, in this time, is clear that I will accompany her on her journey. And 'tis not *Smithfield* that we will travel to." Daniel did not wish to discuss all the details of what he had read of his future in the *Leabhar Sinnsreadh*, but he was quite certain of how it would happen. It felt dangerous to speak of it as if it was some changeable thing, when by all his experience he knew very well that any attempt to alter the future would fail. Even if one managed to change something, time had a way of fixing itself, creating a different way to achieve the same outcome.

"My mother told me as much," Connor admitted. "Something happened to her before we were born and she tried to change things. It took years for her to figure out the consequence of her meddling, and that's why Emmy had to come back. Things need to be set right. Emmy has to be in Smithfield by springtime, or this is all for nothing."

"How far is it from Jamestown?" Daniel asked.

"About twenty miles southeast from the Jamestown settlement. It's not far, even by foot. It's not called Smithfield yet, though. I think it's still part of Basse's Choice until about 1725."

It all fit together at that moment, the once jagged pieces of a puzzle that suddenly merged into one.

Yes, he thought, *so it is true.* Emmy was right when she insisted where she needed to be – and so was Daniel.

"There is not much time to think on it. We are being tracked by Wicawa Ni Tu's men. We must leave this place," Daniel said. He could sit with the man and discuss it for hours, but their time was edging away with each moment of daylight.

"He won't stop. She won't be safe with the Pamunkey. Why should we trust them, or any Indian? They've tried to wipe out our kind once before – I know that Opechancanough killed the Time Walkers that once lived here. They were your family, weren't they?" Connor replied, his words laced with frustration.

"My family still lives, and we have had no quarrel with the Powhatan tribes since the days of my boyhood. It is the Ricahecrians who heard tales and saw your mark. Wicawa Ni Tu does not understand how to work the magic," Daniel said. "I will take you both to the Pamunkey, and then I will meet Wicawa Ni Tu. I owe him a debt and I must see it satisfied. It is the only way to end it."

Daniel spoke the words, the thought of what it might cost him like a heavy mantle upon his back. No, Wicawa Ni Tu would not stop, and there was no other way for Daniel to keep Emmy safe. His only chance was to somehow speak reason to the warrior – and if he failed, at least Emmy would be safe on fortified Pamunkey lands that were granted protection by the Governor of Virginia and the English King.

Emmy and Keke returned with firewood, and Daniel worked to pack their scattered supplies. He listened as Emmy engaged in playful banter with her brother, letting her have a bit of peace before they must leave, for he feared that her time with her brother would not be long.

THE PAMUNKEY OPENED their gates to the weary travelers as dusk settled down over the treetops, and the Elders were notified of their arrival. Activity in the village seemed muted since his last visit, and it was with sorrow that Daniel realized it was the absence of warriors that marked the change. What had happened to those brave men was a tale that Daniel did not wish to relive, but for his cousin, wife to Totopotomoi, and for all the women who lost husbands, he steeled himself to carry the news.

Eager women and children surrounded them. Daniel lost himself in the flurry of attention, allowing them to drape him with gifts of long beaded necklaces and offerings of food. Emmy was treated with great respect, and he loved the way her smile shined across her heart-shaped face as she graciously accepted her gifts. He watched her stay close to her brother, her hair streaming down her back and whipping gently in the early evening breeze, and he ached for the time that he might hold her in his arms once more.

How had she become so important to him, when he had only known her from the words of a book? For all of his life he had known her name, yet the taste of the reality of her was like the power of the rising sun. It surged to rise, swallowing the darkness of the night sky, burning brightly until one had no choice but to welcome it. If she was his destiny, then he was her servant, and he would gladly give the remainder of his days to live in her light.

No matter what was to come, he would fight for her. He would fight to keep her safe, and he would fight to see her on her journey.

When the Pamunkey woman tapped his elbow and summoned him to Cockacoeske, Daniel's eyes searched Emmy's across the crowd. Her smile dimmed and he suspected she knew what he must do, but he turned to his task without hesitation.

"*Cocacoeske* is ready to hear you," the woman intoned, her accent thick with her Pamunkey spoken words. Daniel looked up at the Great Longhouse, pausing at the open door. It was fashioned with a wood frame and shingled roof, still bright and new without the gray aged patina that most of the longhouses in the village displayed.

Cockacoeske's husband, Totopotomoi, was the son of an English Lord and a sister of old Chief Powhatan, and in the years that he ruled the Pamunkey there had been many changes. He negotiated a truce with the Virginia Governor to secure lands for the tribe along the banks of the river on the middle peninsula, surrounding the spot near the river where Opecacanough had reburied Chief Powhatan's bones in a sacred mound. Although it was considered Indiantown, the influence of English cultures was evident, and for the most part there was little conflict between the two groups. Daniel spent three summers there as a boy, learning the old ways and absorbing the language, yet never truly feeling that he belonged. It was not until he was older and grew to know Totopotomoi that Daniel realized he could make his own path, living as a part of both worlds.

He was ushered into a great common room, where Cockacoeske was waiting to receive him. To each side of her stood two young armed warriors, who he recognized as barely a summer older than the *huskanaw* to proclaim them men. She sat upon a carved wood chair with a fat velvet cushion, likely an extravagant gift from the English, and she looked somehow older than he recalled, her face drawn and peaked with strain. Dressed simply in a white doeskin dress and adorned with only a single long strand of freshwater pearls around her neck, she gazed at Daniel with a look of surprise. Daniel kneeled before her, waiting until she invited him to speak.

"Leave us," she commanded, standing up from her chair. The two guards obeyed, and as they closed the door to the long house and left them alone, Cocacoeske came to Daniel and urged him to stand with gentle hands. "I feared you were dead, cousin," she said. "Tell me, where is my husband? Why do you walk alone?" Her eyes held the sorrow of what he was sure she already suspected, and he could think of nothing to comfort her, even if he had means to comfort a woman who was now the ruler of the Pamunkey.

"I am sorry," he said softly. He wanted to bow his head but he felt that he owed her the honesty of his gaze, so he fixed his eyes on hers. "We were told the Governor wished for a peaceable resolution with the Ricahecrians. Colonel Hill slaughtered five of their chiefs and he withdrew the Colonial Militia."

"He left the Pamunkey to fight alone?"

Daniel nodded. "Yes. We were one hundred strong, but it was not enough. We were outnumbered. Totopotomoi fought until the end, and now his spirit soars in the light of the Great Creator."

She said nothing, her body stiff as a plank and her gaze suddenly hollowed. Her skin flushed deep scarlet from the base of her neck to the rounds of her cheeks, and for a long moment he thought she did not breathe. He could smell the heavy scent of sap tree wood that burned in the hearth fire as he inhaled which made his nose burn, and it reminded him of the burial ceremony that would soon commence. He almost reached out to her for fear she might fall, but she stepped back and calmly sat down on her chair.

"And all of our warriors?" she finally asked.

"They died fighting," he said. Her fingers clenched the arms of her chair and her knuckles stood out like a row of white pearls.

"I see. Did you speak with their chief before they attacked? The Ricahercrians are still a problem to us all, even if the English chose to run instead of fight."

"Yes, I reached an agreement with their War Chief, Wicawa Ni Tu. I believe he is of Manahoac blood, as he speaks that tongue, but he is the leader of all the Ricahecrians."

She dipped her head slightly, urging him to continue. "And the agreement?"

Daniel sighed. He did not wish to convey the details of the interaction, but if she asked it of him he had no choice.

"He held a Time Walker as a prisoner. The Time Walker was not one I recognized, and he was not of my uncle's family. Wicawa Ni Tu said the man had a woman somewhere nearby, and he asked me to bring the woman to him. I agreed to the bargain, but it was then that Colonel Hill slaughtered the five chiefs, and the battle started."

"So this Time Walker is important to Wicawa Ni Tu. Do you know where she may be found?" she asked.

It was the question he feared she would ask.

"She is with me," he replied. "We are being tracked. I killed one of Wicawa Ni Tu's scouts."

"Good. Take her to them, and end this. Perhaps it will quell Wicawa Ni Tu's thirst for vengeance. We cannot rely on the word of the English to see our people safe. I see no other way to keep peace, and we have no more warriors to spare."

Daniel felt as if the earth dropped away beneath his feet. He brought Emmy to his cousin for protection, not to turn her over to their enemy.

"Forgive me, cousin, but that is something I cannot do," he said. "For she is mine and our path is already decided by the Book of the Blooded Ones."

Cockacoeske's eyes widened. "So you would disobey me?"

"I do not wish to disobey you, so I ask that you do not command me to do so. I am loyal to your people, the same as I am to the kinsmen of my uncle. Yet I will protect her with my dying breath, and if I must be punished for my disobedience, then I will gladly submit to your will."

He kneeled down before her and bowed his head, his hands tight at his sides. "I stood beside Topotomoi, and I know he fought to come back to you. I know the emptiness you hold in your heart for his death. Do not ask me to disobey you. Do not ask me to give what I cannot give." His pulse pounded in his ears in the long silence that followed, and all he could think of was how he would get Emmy out of the village if Cockacoeske denied his request.

"I thank you for carrying this message. Leave me now, cousin. We will speak more on this in the light of the morning," she said.

Daniel obeyed. As he was leaving, he glanced back at her. Her hands gripped the arms of her chair, and although she sat upright and stiff and her eyes were tightly closed, tears streamed silently down her cheeks.

HE FOUND EMMY in the crowd some time later. She sat with the women of the village, nibbling on a bit of crusted bread and taking sips of drink from a wooden cup. They were a few men standing nearby who playfully tried to get the attention of the women, making a game of tossing pebbles at them. Although he did not care to see her enjoy the attention of the young warriors who surrounded her, he was relieved to see her happy and safe. There was no shortage of admirers, however, and when she threw her head back and laughed and he could see the outline of her pale neck illuminated in the glow of the sunlight, he wanted to kill the men who were lucky enough to be at her side. Fortunately, he recognized that jealousy was not an admirable trait and he chose to keep his frustration to himself.

Despite his desire to be near her, he noticed that Connor was missing, so he set out to the medicine house to find him.

"Greetings, friend," he said to the guard in their own tongue. The guard nodded in return, maintaining his authoritative stance without wavering. He was a young man, likely no more than thirteen summers old, and once again the loss of the Pamunkey warriors hit him in the gut. *How would they survive, with so few grown men and so many women and children to look after?*

Inside he found Connor lying flat on a long platform, the *kwiocosuk* at his side. It had been many years since he watched the *kwiocosuk* work, but he was still fascinated by the act of healing. Before Daniel was born the rituals were considered so sacred that only other *kwiocosuks* or Weroances were permitted to be present. After years of cohabitation and subsequent merging of cultures with the English settlers, however, many of the traditional customs within the Indian community changed.

Smoke billowed up in a twisting pattern to the hole at the top of the long house from the handful of tightly bound dried roots that the medicine man held. He was an elder *kwiocosuk*, with his head plucked completely bare except for a small swatch of hair in the middle that stood upright, stiffened and shiny from the bear grease used to keep it in place. Unlike the red vermillion paint the warriors wore, the medicine man painted his face and chest black, and his eyes stood out like bright little moon globes on his dark face.

The medicine man chanted in the language of the ancients, asking the Great Spirit Okee to heal the man's wounds. With each pause in his song he waved the bundle of dried burning roots in a circular motion over Connor to invite the healing smoke into the wound, then waved his hands upward to drive the tainted smoke up toward the smoke hole, releasing the heat from the body to banish the sickness. When he was finished he stomped the tiny root torch out with his foot, completing the healing ritual.

"The blood is tainted with stagger grass. I can do no more for him. I have asked the Great Spirit Okee to take his sickness, but this man has gone many days with this wound," the *kwiocosuk* said.

Daniel suspected that the Ricahecrians dipped their arrow tips in poison, as Connor's wound held a distinct odor and spider-web streaked appearance. It was a particularly harsh way to punish one's enemies well after a battle was over. The Pamunkey used stagger grass to kill off crows in their newly seeded corn fields, and as a child he recalled helping the women remove the dead birds from the fields. There was enough poison in the bulb of the white stagger grass flower to kill an animal in a few hours; how long a man would suffer was another matter.

"Thank you," Daniel replied, tilting his head downward in respect. The medicine man left the dwelling, as he did not often stray far from his *quiocosin* where he lived alone and apart from the other Pamunkey.

Connor tried to sit up on the table. Daniel took his arm and helped him rise, studying the wound on the man's shoulder. Although it was cleaned and the wound itself was mostly closed, the stench still emanated from it, accompanied by a trickle of green-tinged fluid.

"Perhaps the ritual will help," Daniel said quietly.

Connor uttered a deep sigh. "There's no changing this. It's infected and I can feel I'm starting to get a fever. You know it, and I know it. I guess the guys who wrote that fucking book forgot to mention I'd suffer for weeks before I died," Connor said. He grabbed his shirt and pulled it on, covering the evidence of his affliction with the buckskin vest and long coat.

"When I left Basse's Choice, my cousin's wife was near the time to birth her child. The child surely is born by now, or else will be soon. 'Tis a day's trip by foot," Daniel said. He knew it was not his right to barter with the newborn's blood, but he also knew that his cousin would understand.

"I won't make it that far. My fate is set," Connor replied. "My mother tried her best to change things, but some things are not meant to change. You know, Emmy was supposed to come here with a vial of her blood."

"Her blood?" Daniel asked, leaning back on the table and crossing his arms.

"Yeah. My mother secured a bit of my sister's newborn blood in a vial, like she had been taught to do by her own mother. But once she found the book, she made the mistake of reading the *Leabhar Sinnsreadh*. And then she made an even bigger mistake by trying to change things. She read about my death in the past, so

173

she made sure Emmy kept it with her. My mother wanted Emmy to use it to heal me when the time came. The only problem is that she used it to bring me back to life in the future."

"So if your mother changed things, then it is possible," Daniel offered, wanting to know the truth of it even beyond the thought of helping Connor.

"I think so," Connor replied. "I've been trying to figure it all out in my head. From what I know, you can change something that has not happened yet, but if you try to change an event that already happened – like Emmy and my mother did – time will eventually set itself right."

"It makes my head hurt to think on it," Daniel admitted, trying to grasp the meaning of Connor's words. "You think changing the past is impossible, but changing the future is not?"

"Exactly. My mother brought us to the future. She read about my death in the past and she thought she could prevent it with Emmy's infant blood. But by the time she did that in the future, I had already died in the past. So time ripples, and some other event happened to set it all straight again – hence, the day I was shot and killed in the future."

"What meaning is *ripples*?"

Connor shrugged. "It was something my mother always said whenever we'd get déjà vu, you know, that weird feeling you have when you think you've been somewhere before? She called them ripples, and she said it happened whenever something changed in your timeline. I used to get it a lot when I was a kid, so I'm guessing whatever my mother did screwed up my destiny pretty good."

Daniel thought over the explanation. He had never experienced the feeling Connor described, but Daniel recalled his cousin, Dagr, complain of something similar when they were children.

Connor ran his hand over his brow, wiping away the sweat on his skin. Daniel suspected it would not be long before the man could no longer function. It seemed an act of pure willpower that he still managed at all, considering that fever was starting to take hold.

"I need to ask you to do something for me," Connor said, his voice strangely calm. "I need you to take care of my sister when the time comes. She will fight you, you know. But you must not let it sway you. Give her this, and she will understand."

Connor unsheathed the knife at his side and handed it to Daniel. It was the blade of a Chief Protector, meant to be held by those who made the life vow to protect the Blooded Ones at all cost. His uncle and cousin each held one, and Daniel knew what it meant to carry such a weapon. A Bloodstone was embedded in the hilt and rune carvings circled the finely worked handle. It felt heavy in his hand when he took it, from the weight of weapon or the burden of the duty it carried, he did not know.

Connor then held his hand out and Daniel accepted it, making a promise to the man with clasped arms.

"I will. Above all else, I will protect her," Daniel promised.

"Thank you," Connor replied. "This is what we will do …"

13

Emmy

"I DON'T UNDERSTAND," Emmy said, crossing her arms over her chest. She watched as Daniel gathered his pack, her frustration rising by the minute.

"It is how they mourn. The women must stay in their long houses, alone, and sing the mourning song," Daniel explained. He placed one hand on her cheek and kissed her gently on the lips. "It is not my choice to be parted, even for one night."

"How long will it last?" she asked.

"Through the night, you will hear the songs, and in the morning there will be a celebration of life. The *kwiocosuk* will usually prepare the body to lay with the great Weroances in the sacred *quiocosin*, but they will forgo that for now since we have not recovered Totopotomoi's body."

He bowed his head, resting it against hers for a moment, and when he drew away she did not miss the unease in his eyes. Daniel was a complicated man and she thought she knew him by now, but the look on his face was one she had never witnessed. *Was he mourning the loss of Totopotomoi, or was it something more?* Even when they fled from the cottage under the threat of being followed, Daniel had not appeared so forlorn, so his current demeanor was puzzling to her.

"What is it, Daniel?" she asked. "What troubles you?"

"Nothing for you to worry on," he replied. He picked up his satchel and hoisted it over his shoulder. "You should visit with your brother before the songs begin. He is in the medicine house."

It was then that she saw it again, the strain in his face, and as he left her she wondered if it had something to do with Connor.

Emmy looked up at the sky. She had some time before sunset, so she set out to see her brother.

SHE FOUND HIM sitting upright on a platform cot, his eyes closed as if he were sleeping. A thin layer of sweat shined on his skin and his breathing was rapid and shallow. She hoped that he would start to recover soon, worried that he seemed to be getting worse rather than better.

"Hey," she said softly, sitting down next to him. He opened his eyes and smiled.

"Hey, sis," he replied. He shifted and sat up more, grimacing as he put pressure on his left hand.

"What's going on, Connor? Why is Daniel so tense, and what else are you two not telling me?"

Connor sighed. He was freshly bathed and it appeared that he wore a new white cotton trade shirt beneath his vest.

"I'm just tired, that's all. And worried about the Ricahecrians," he replied. Emmy wasn't sure she believed his explanation, and she could not suppress her rising suspicion.

"If you say so," she added.

"There is something I need to talk to you about, though," Conner said. "Do you remember when we were kids, and mother told us the truth? You know, the day she sat us down at the kitchen table and told us we were Blooded Ones?"

Emmy uttered a half-snort, half-laugh. Of course she remembered it. She was eight years old and it was the day her entire world changed. From that day on, life in the twenty-first century did not matter, it was just a ruse of a life while she grew older and prepared for what would come.

"Sometimes I wish she never told us," she confessed.

"That's a little harsh. She was doing what she thought was right."

She shrugged, trying to figure out the words to make him understand. "You were older. It was different for you, like some adventure. But after that day, I never felt like I belonged anywhere. I was only eight years old, Connor," she explained. "And my mother is telling me I have some immense duty to travel through time and fix things? I don't know what she did to screw things up, or why she did it, but why should I have to clean up her mess? Why is it all on my shoulders?"

"She never meant any of this to happen. She had her own demons to deal with. You think you had it rough? Mom lived in the fifteenth century and she was a prisoner her entire life until father saved her. It's only because of what they did that you and I had a normal life in the future. They did it to save us, and we can't turn our backs on them now."

She swallowed hard, biting back a sharp retort. He was right, and she felt like a spoiled child for even verbalizing her scattered thoughts. "I'm not turning my back on them. I'll do what I'm supposed to do. I don't know what will happen when I get to Smithfield, but I'll still go."

He placed his hand over hers and squeezed it. "I know you will. And that's what I need to talk to you about. You still have the book, right?"

"Of course I do. And speaking of the book, why did mother have it? She told us that only one of the Five Northmen held it – a Chief Protector."

"When you were about five, mother had a vision about the book. It led her to an antique bookstore in the old town section of Philly and she found it there. She knew there was no way that book would ever leave the hands of the Chief, unless something awful had happened. That's when she read it and realized she must send you to the past. And it was hard on her, the knowing, that is. She didn't handle it well. It destroyed her."

"Why didn't she ever tell me this? Why were you her only confidant?" Emmy asked. It sounded spiteful but that was not her intent.

"Because she knew what it felt like to know when she would die. She read it, she read all of it, and she knew every detail. She didn't know if it was better to prepare you for your future, or if she should just let fate happen and let you figure it all out on your own someday."

"Daniel read it, too. I know it haunts him," she said softly. Connor nodded.

"Yeah, so she did what she thought was best. She told me enough to help you prepare, but after she died, I read the book. Technically, I was the closest thing to a Chief Protector, and I figured I had a right to know if I was charged with guarding the damn thing."

"So tell me what it said," she replied. *Didn't she have a right to know all the details?*

"You know I won't do that, Em," he said quietly. "You'll go to Smithfield, and they'll be expecting you. If you open the book, about half way through you'll find a page with a folded pocket. There's a letter in there with a wax seal. If you think you'll be tempted to read the book, have Daniel retrieve it for you. Trust me on this, Emmy."

"What does the letter say?" she asked.

"I don't know. It's addressed to you and the wax seal is intact. Once you see it, you'll know when it's time to open it."

She contemplated that notion for a moment. A sealed letter addressed to her? How could that be, and when did it get placed into the *Leabhar Sinnsreadh?*

"Okay," she said. "I'll do it."

There was nothing else she could say that made any sense. The reality of her duty hit her hard once more, knowing that what was to come was bigger than her or Connor or any one person.

"Go on, now," Connor said, leaning his head back. "You need to get back to your longhouse before the ritual starts."

She stood up and kissed his clammy cheek. "I'll see you tomorrow."

He muttered something under his breath as she left, and if she did not know him any better she would have thought he said, *"I love you, sis."*

She returned to her empty longhouse. It was not long afterward that the mourning song began. It was one sorrowful voice in the beginning, joined every few minutes by another, until the starless night was filled with the woeful keening of every widowed woman in the village. Emmy did not understand the words to the song, but even without that knowledge the grief-stricken voices rang clear.

Tonight was for the fallen Weroance, a man beloved by his people. But there would be many more nights of keening for the one hundred warriors lost that day by his side, and the thought of that sorrow humbled Emmy as she laid awake that night and listened.

THE NIGHT OF mourning was over. A life celebration ritual immediately commenced and the people prepared for a feast, cooking a large boar on a spit over the village fire. Thick smoke billowed up and filled the air, heavy with traces of oak chip scent and roasted meat.

She did not see Daniel until late morning, and only then it was by spotting him with the other men. It frustrated her to be away from him. She wondered if he would be permitted to share the long house with her that evening, or if they would need to sleep separately while they were in the village. The Indians certainly had no qualms about sex or unmarried men and women sharing a bed, as she had seen more than one episode of blatant sexual activity in the secluded areas of the village since she arrived. Whatever the reason, the situation was out of her control and she didn't like it one bit.

"Miss Cameron," a young man said in hesitant English. She recognized him as one of the warriors who stood outside the Great Long House where the Chief and his wife resided, which sadly, was now only for Cockacoeske.

"My *Weroansqua* seeks your presence in the Great *Yehakin*," he said without preamble. She followed him without question, knowing that any sort of response to object would be considered an insult, and that was the last thing she wished to convey.

Cockacoeske was alone inside when she entered the long house. The new Queen was adorned with very few trinkets, which surprised Emmy since many of the Weroances enjoyed showing off their wealth for visitors. Yet Cockacoeske was a different sort, a product of the old ways merged with a growing tolerance of the new, and in her lifetime the culture of the English settlers had merged with those of the Pamunkey people. Emmy was not sure how to greet her properly, so she assumed a subservient position by kneeling down on one knee with her head lowered in respect.

"Rise, Time Walker," the Weroansqua said.

So at least that was out of the way, Emmy thought. *She knows what I am.*

"Thank you," Emmy replied, raising her head and standing upright. It was impossible to tell what the Queen was thinking by the neutral mask on her face. Smoke from the low banked fire was thick in the long house, and as Emmy approached she could feel a sting in her eyes and taste the heaviness of burnt wood bark in her mouth just from breathing the air. The Queen, however, seemed unaffected, and Emmy choked back a cough instead of appearing weak to the powerful woman in front of her.

"This morning we captured a Ricahecrian warrior who came inside our palisades," Cockacoeske said. She flicked her wrist and waved at a thick purple cushion on the floor beside her chair, indicating that Emmy should sit, so she obeyed even though panicked thoughts were sifting through her mind.

"They took my brother prisoner, and they were tracking Daniel," Emmy offered.

"No," the Queen said. "They are tracking *you*. It is your blood they want, that power in your veins. Daniel promised their War Chief a woman Time Walker in exchange for peace. If I give you and your brother to them, it will end this bloody war that has already taken our bravest warriors. What say you?"

Emmy's fingers wrapped tight on the edge of the velvet cushion beneath her, gripping it to steady herself. *No. Daniel would not betray them. He would not betray her.*

"Daniel brought us here for protection," she said. The words came out clear despite her unease. The Queen looked hard at Emmy, her disposition unreadable, and it took everything Emmy had to simply wait for the Queen to respond.

"So he did," the Queen agreed. "Do you know who Daniel is to me?"

"I know he is your kinsman, but nothing more."

Emmy was relieved to see a softening in the Queen's body as the conversation turned. Cockacoeske's shoulders relaxed a bit as she let out a long breath.

"He is the son of my cousin, Winkeohkwet, but he was fathered by my cousin Makedewa," she said, her voice betraying a touch of whimsical remembrance. "He favors Winkeohkwet in many ways, but I see more of his blood father in him now than in all the years I have known him. He never knew Makedewa, but I did."

It seemed the Queen was immersed in the telling of a story, so Emmy gave her the respect of her silence and tried to make sense of it all as she continued her tale.

"Makedewa was a brave man who lived his days haunted by his hatred for the English. Once he took an English wife his hatred dimmed, but it returned once more when she died. It was then that I knew him, when he served to protect Opechancanough. To Opechancanough, this hatred was good. It made Makedewa a strong warrior," she said. "Yet I see it in another way. I see a man who was first blinded by his love for his English wife, and then I see a man who was blinded by grief. I look at Daniel now and I see much of Makedewa in him. So it is why I ask you now, as you sit at my feet, what path we must take. Should I give the Ricahecrian War Chief what he was promised?"

What answer could she give? And what did the Queen want to hear?

"You know what we are. You know what we can do. My people have been hunted for centuries because of the selfish desires of powerful men," Emmy replied evenly. "There are few of my kind left."

"I can say the same for what is left of my people," the Queen said curtly. "Tell me, why my cousin protects you."

"Because our path has been foretold in the Book of the Blooded Ones. We cannot change that. Even if we try,

184

time seeks a way to right it somehow. Daniel knows that, as do I."

"So you give Daniel the power to control your destiny?"

Emmy nodded. "I trust him with my life. I know he would never harm me, nor would he ever try to use my power for selfish means."

"Wicawa Ni Tu wants to heal the sickness in his people. Is that a selfish thing?"

"No, that is not selfish. But what he did to my brother and what he would do to me is different. We cannot heal the sick or dead with a few drops of our blood; it is only by draining my life blood that my brother or I could save a life. Wicawa Ni Tu does not understand the magic, nor the consequence of what he asks."

"Why not tell him? Show him how the magic works. I know it can heal the dead. Makedewa was said to have died, yet he was restored by a Blooded One and lived for many years."

Emmy met her gaze. To tell the truth of how it worked was something she swore she would never share with an outsider. It was the reason her kind had been hunted for hundreds of years, the reason why even her mother had suffered. Yet there was nothing else Emmy could do to pacify Cockacoeske, and if she did not give the Queen what she wanted, then they were as good as dead anyway.

"Most of my kind have the power to Time Travel," Emmy said quietly. "But it is the newborn children that have the power to heal the sick and dead. A simple prick of the heel and a few drops of blood will restore life. Children lose the healing power once they are past a year old. So a Blooded woman is of high value – until she can

185

no longer bear children. Once that time comes, her only value is in her death."

Cockacoeske seemed to consider her words for some time before she spoke again. When the Queen reached for the Bloodstone on Emmy's neck, Emmy took it off and handed it to her. There was no reason to deny her curiosity; they were well past any way to deny what was said.

"And this is the stone you use to travel?" she asked, turning the greenish-black stone over in her hands, studying the red veins running through it. It was set into a gold base, attached to a rawhide cord, and had been a gift from her mother on her tenth birthday. It was only then that mother felt Emmy was responsible enough to hold it, and mother explained that for centuries their kind always carried a Bloodstone in one form or another. For Connor, it was his father's knife with a Bloodstone embedded in the hilt.

"Yes," Emmy replied, holding out her left hand, palm upraised, so that the Queen could see her scar. "It marked me when I traveled here. Time has a way of setting things right, even when men have manipulated it by controlling the Blooded Ones. There is always a consequence to using the power."

The Queen tilted her head slightly to the side as if to study Emmy, her dark eyes searching Emmy's face.

"If you can change the truth of your past and choose what should begin and what should never be, tell me, now, how one might wield that power, or how it might be meant for one man's whim," Cockacoeske said.

"The danger to my kind, and the danger to all people – that is why we stay hidden. That is why the Five Northmen joined with the Five Chiefs and made a vow to

186

protect the magic. That is why I am here in this time, to set things right."

The Queen rose from her chair. She held the Bloodstone out to Emmy, dangling it from her fingers. Emmy closed her hand around the stone, feeling the warmth of it, and she placed it back around her neck where it belonged.

"I thank you for your counsel," Cockacoeske said. "And I grant you my protection. Join the others now for a celebration of life, and see how they speak kindly of my husband, who was a great man."

Emmy nodded in gratitude, bowing to the Queen before she left.

MEN AND WOMEN danced around the fire, and despite her rising frustration with being away from Daniel, Emmy laughed when one of the men took her hand and brought her into the circle. She did not know the steps to the dance, but she gave it her best shot, stumbling through the motions to the bemusement of onlookers.

Emmy twirled in the arms of the warrior, laughing as he guided her through the steps of the celebration dance. His name was Catakwa and she judged that he was about her age, and although he was tattooed and painted red in the style of a warrior, she knew that he had not fought in the battle at the Falls since all those warriors were slain.

Across the fire, Daniel stood with other men, yet his gaze was fixed on her and it brought a flush of warmth to her skin. The distance seemed like nothing when the power of his eyes could touch her so far away.

When Catakwa placed a hand on her waist, she saw the darkness descend on Daniel's face. *Perhaps he felt the strain of their separation as much as she did*, she thought. It had been almost two long days since they had been alone and she suspected it affected him as much as it did her. Did he miss her as much as she missed him?

Away from the fire, a crowd of men made a half-circle, and one of them called for Catakwa. She was relieved for the interlude, as she did not want the attentions of anyone except Daniel, but she was intrigued when the men pushed Catakwa into the middle of the circle and roared with laughter. She pushed through the crowd to get a glimpse, wondering just exactly what sort of game they had planned for the warrior.

It was not long before Daniel stepped forward, his eyes fixed intently on Catakwa. She felt like the earth plummeted away from her feet as they circled each other and the men began to shout, rousing a rhythmical chant to provoke what might come.

"What are they doing?" Emmy asked, nudging a young woman who stood next to her. The woman shrugged.

"They fight to see who will bed the women. They are stupid," the woman muttered.

"What?" Emmy shot back. "Wait a second. I'm not bedding anyone, I don't care if they beat each other to a bloody pulp!"

The woman laughed, shaking her head. "No, not you. *Them.*" She pointed across the circle to a pair of women standing apart from the others. They were tall and they looked like twins, matched in every way from the length of their long dark hair down to the tips of their lean legs.

He was fighting over them? Surely the woman was mistaken.

She raised her drink to her lips and took a long swallow of it. She wasn't sure of what exactly it was, but she suspected it was some sort of alcohol and she welcomed the bitter numbness that went down her throat. Getting tipsy was one way to get through watching him fight.

"Just what in God's name do you think you're doing, Daniel?" she muttered under her breath.

The two men locked arms, grappling with heads down. They seemed of equal strength and size, but neither had the upper hand as they both managed to stay upright. She winced when Catakwa brought Daniel to the ground. Closing her eyes to the fight, she tried to wait it out, yet the grunts and shouts from the men were even worse than simply watching. When she opened her eyes, the situation was reversed and Daniel was on top of Catakwa.

At that moment Daniel looked like a vengeful pagan god, streaked with red paint from his opponent and dripping with sweat. He stood up slowly, his bare chest rising and falling with each rapid breath, the gleam of fierce confidence blazing in his eyes. When his eyes met hers it sent a shiver down her spine, speaking to her in a way that words never could.

She pushed through the crowd to reach him, threading through the throng of painted women and children. When she had nearly reached him, she stopped short and froze, ignoring those who shouldered into her as if she were alone in the village.

The two women were with Daniel. One of the women rested her hand on Daniel's bare chest, while the

189

other looped her arm through his. Daniel was still flushed and breathing heavily from the fight, but he seemed to be tolerating the attention until his eyes met hers.

"Emmy," he called out. He twisted away from the women and approached her, but she had seen enough.

She tore her eyes from his and turned away, her fists clenched at her sides. *Let him have those women,* she fumed. *If he needed to prove his manhood so badly, so be it.*

The longhouse Cockacoeske granted her was not far. When she reached it she slammed the door shut and threw her cloak over a chair, taking off her boots and tossing them in the corner for good measure. Well, he had another thing coming, because she wasn't going to accept that in his century or any other. She did her duty and stayed alone in the long house just as he insisted she do, and then she managed to change the mind of the Queen and save all of their skins. *Was this what her life would be like someday as Daniel's wife? Watching in silence as she did her duty and he paraded women in front of her face?*

She recognized her jealousy for what it was – purely irrational and likely unwarranted – yet, still, it infuriated her and she could not get the image of that woman's hand on Daniel out of her mind. She knew some of the Pamunkey men kept multiple wives, yet she did not think that was how Daniel was raised. Did he think so little of her that he thought she would tolerate such a thing?

Daniel opened the door a moment later, slamming it shut with such force that she feared it would snap off the hinges. He dropped the plank into place and she

190

swallowed hard, feeling her heart stuck in her throat at the feral look in his eyes.

"Enjoy your fight?" she asked boldly.

He said nothing at first, approaching her slowly as if she were his prey, her heart racing like a jackrabbit caught in a snare. She backed up away from him, shaking her head as if to stir him, anything she could do to change the mask of raw depravity on his face.

"Well, while you men spent all day fighting to figure out who had bigger balls, I was brought to the Queen," she stammered. He raised a brow but remained silent, his chest heaving with the force of his breathing. "She wanted to give me to the Ricahecrians. Both me and my brother. I talked to her – I convinced her not to do it."

"Oh?" he said, as if she had only announced a casual conversation instead of avoidance of certain death.

"*Oh?*" she hissed. "That's all you have to say? *Oh?*"

"Yes. And I am weary and want my woman to welcome me to her furs."

"Where are your women?" she asked, stepping backward. He continued to stalk her, his dark eyes fixed on hers, his breath shallow. He took his tunic off, lifting it swiftly over his head before he tossed it to the floor, the lines of his chest standing out like finely sculpted carvings wrought on stone. Sweat dappled his brow and blood dripped from a scrape on his chest, but he was otherwise unharmed. When her eyes drifted downward she could see exactly what he wanted, and it took all of her self-control to keep from fleeing when he closed the space between them.

"My *woman*," he said, his voice no more than a low rolling growl, "is right here. It has been too long since I have touched her, and I plan to remedy that fact now."

"Don't come to me after you've fought over another woman. I won't have you," she said, her voice steady although her breathing was rapid. "I don't believe in sharing. I believe in – in *monogamy*."

"I fought for *you*. I watched Catakwa dance with you all day. I watched a man put his hands on what belongs to me. Did you think that would not stir me, or that I would not call him out?" Daniel replied darkly. His fists tightened and his veins stood out like ropes on his flesh. He was breathing as hard as she was, and she could see he was about to lose what little restraint he had left.

"Did you forget who you belonged to when Catakwa whispered in your ear?" he asked.

She stared defiantly back at him. *So he was jealous, too.* Her back hit the cold stone of the wall and he took advantage of her position, trapping her with his hands on each side.

"You don't own me," she whispered. "If you can let some woman fawn all over you, I can talk to a man, just the same." The instant the words left her lips she knew it was the wrong thing to say, and suddenly the glare in his eyes assured her that he would prove her wrong.

His mouth crashed down on hers and his hands sought her chemise, tearing it downward to shed it from her body. She raised her hands in protest, pushing him away, but his body was hard steel pressed against her and there was no denying him.

"Stop it," she demanded when his mouth descended to her neck. He shoved her hands above her head, holding her wrists in one hand, his other hand working to open his breeches.

"Are you not mine?" he asked, his voice hoarse and his mouth pressed against her ear. "Tell me. Tell me you are not."

She shuddered when his hungry mouth lowered and closed over her nipple, sucking hard on one as he stroked the other breast. What were they fighting over, and why did she taunt him? Was it the frustration of their situation, or the simple power of what they were to each other? It was a truth neither could deny; he set her to flame as surely as the sun rose in the sky each day. Be it some primal desire or an ancient prophecy, it did not matter. She belonged to him, and she would refuse him no longer.

"Daniel," she moaned. "I am yours. I am yours." He lifted her off the ground and spread her legs, sinking fully into her with one swift thrust. She cried out, her breath leaving her lungs each time he surged into her, pushing her upward against the wall with each measured stroke. He was unrestrained and raw, slating his lust, and when he drew back and looked into her eyes it made her blood burn in her veins. When he let go of her wrists her hands slipped down and twisted into his hair, clutching him to her while he gripped her hips and drove home.

"*Nowami*," he breathed, his words hot on her ear. "You. Are. Mine."

Afterward, he laid her down on the furs and made love to her again, and although her body was sore, her soul was satiated, and she welcomed him until he was spent of his need. Nothing could have prepared her for the intensity of his touch, or the way he refused to stop until she screamed his name and begged for release. He was a man driven by need, yet she knew that her own surge of petty jealousy was nothing compared to the raw possession her felt for her.

In the hours of darkness before the dawn, he held her tightly against his chest, his lips pressed into her hair. She could not move if she had wanted to, and it was there in his arms with their limbs entwined that she knew she would always be safe.

"I wanted you before I knew you, before I ever looked into your eyes or touched your body," he said softly. "I knew your heart was mine, that I must wait for it, and that once you knew it too, I would never let you go."

She clutched her fist to his chest, her lips resting against his skin.

"Don't ever let me go," she whispered.

"Never," he replied. He turned over and pinned her gently into the furs, kissing her chin and jaw and then tracing a path down her neck to her breasts, where he lingered as he gave them his attention. She closed her eyes and let out a sigh, surprised and a little bit disappointed when he suddenly leaned up on his forearms and raised his head.

"Why would I care about the size of balls?" he asked, a wicked gleam in his eyes. "And what does *monogamy* mean?"

She laughed so hard that she snorted, and it was several seconds before she could control herself enough to answer.

"Monogamy means you are faithful to one woman," she said. "And these are your *balls*," she giggled, cupping

194

her hand between his thighs in demonstration. His eyes widened and his face broke into a grin.

"Oh, those," he said with a dismissive tone, dipping his lips to her cheek. He kissed her softly and she squirmed when she felt his teeth tug at her earlobe. "I have no desire to compare balls, nor will I ever share you with another."

She writhed and ached her back, trying to get her ear away from his seeking mouth. "It means I won't share you, either!" she laughed. She tried to put on her most serious face but failed miserably.

He held her tight and met her gaze, a boyish grin upon his lips. "I know. You are too busy pleasing me to have time for any other," he said. "And I plan to keep you like that."

With that declaration, he shifted over and pushed his knee between her legs to part her thighs, and showed her exactly how he would keep her occupied.

14

Daniel

HE FOUND HER that morning with a few of the village women that she had somehow convinced to help her prepare a travois. Although Emmy knew few Pamunkey words, some of the Indian women knew a bit of English, and they stumbled through communicating with a mixture of short phrases and gestures. He could not help but smile when he approached and saw Emmy pointing at a small pile of braided reed twine, then holding her hands palm up to indicate she needed more.

She was dressed in her tight blue trousers topped with an overly large white shirt which was held in place by a leather belt, and he could see she had acquired a new harness similar to the one that Ahi Kekeleksu wore to carry his sword. Her long hair was braided and tucked neatly over one shoulder, and she wore tall leather boots that shined and reflected in the rays of the early morning sun when she moved.

Daniel did not particularly mind the odd garments she wore, and truth be told, it was quite enjoyable to see the soft curves of her body unrestricted by the heavy layers of a dress. He wondered what she would look like dressed in the summer attire of a Pamunkey woman and it brought a surge of warmth to his chest as he pictured her that way, clad only in a doeskin skirt with a loose mantle covering her breasts.

"What are you doing?" he asked. She was kneeling on the travois, tying off a knot where she mended a frayed edge. Looking at her and the way she made friends with the women intrigued him. *Was there any place where she would not fit in?* Despite his suspicions that her upbringing had been traumatic, she was a woman who knew how to get what she wanted and who was prepared to work hard to achieve it.

"Connor is not much better. I think we might need to carry him to Basse's Choice. You said your cousin's wife was ready to give birth. Do you think they would heal him? Connor, I mean. I'm just worried about him," she said. "He's not recovering like he should."

Daniel did not wish to keep anything from her, but his need to keep her safe was greater than his fear of angering her. No, her brother was not going to make the journey to Basse's Choice; in fact, Daniel suspected he would not last until dawn. Before looking for Emmy, Daniel had checked on Connor. The man could no longer move his arms and legs without extreme effort, especially his left shoulder and arm that were closest to his wound. Paralysis was setting in, and from what Daniel knew of the effects of stagger grass poison, it would be much more merciful to end his life now than to allow him to decline any further. Yet Connor was just as stubborn as his sister. He refused Daniel's offer and insisted he would wait for his time.

Yes, she will hate me when it happens, he thought, *but she will be alive, and once she has time to think on it,*

197

she will understand. He knew that truth for certain, but it did not make the task of deceiving her any easier.

"My cousin and his wife will welcome you both," Daniel replied. It was the truth. "But there are things I must tell you before we leave. Will you walk with me?"

She nodded, shoving her hands into the pockets of her trousers as she walked beside him. He took her away from the busy center of the village to a more secluded place by the river, finding that the sounds of seabirds crying out overhead and the rush of the water eased him somewhat in preparation of what he must confess to her.

"Do you see the hills on the ridge downstream?" he asked, pointing in the direction of the sacred burial mounds. He rested one foot on a large rock embedded in the riverbank, watching her as she sheltered her eyes with one flat hand on her brow and stood up on the tips of her toes to look.

"Yes, I see them," she replied. "Burial mounds?"

"Yes. Before the war in 1622, Opechancanough brought Powhatan's bones here to be buried. It is said that Opechancanough felt he must honor his brother before he could continue on to become *Mangopeesomon*, the name he took when he was ready to attack the English."

"I know how that war ended," Emmy said softly.

"As do I," he replied. He let the sharp river air fill his lungs before he continued. It was difficult for him to speak of the father and mother he never knew. Although he always had a place in his uncle's home, Daniel never felt as if he truly belonged to either world. There was nothing left of the Paspahegh people who once had many villages throughout the lands of *Tsenacommacah*, and what life he lived among the English at Basse's Choice was a blending of cultures. Yet he heard other speak of his father, and when they mentioned his name it was a name they said with respect.

"My mother was an English woman," he said quietly. "She was barely more than a child the day the Powhatan attacked Jamestown. They planned it for years and attacked every plantation and town along the river in one day. My father rode with his brothers, my uncles Winn and Chetan, and they were ordered to go into the homes of the English settlers and slaughter them where they stood. Men, women, and children … it was all the same to Opechancanough."

Emmy's eye met his. He reveled in the connection, keeping it close to him, for he feared it would take a long time for her to truly understand.

"My uncles never intended to carry out Opechancanough's orders. Winn was there to save his grandmother and my aunt from the slaughter. My father, however, was not as convinced the English should not all die, as he held a great hatred for them all. It was not until he saw my mother that he could see through his hatred. He killed another warrior to spare my mother, and on that day, he knew she was his. My father knew she had suffered a great loss, as her entire family was killed, yet he had patience in the love he felt for my mother. He waited many years to wed her, remaining her faithful companion until she was ready to be his wife."

"He sounds like an honorable man," Emmy said softly. She reached for him, taking his hand and entwining her fingers with his.

"Perhaps. Some might believe he only waited for my mother, so that in the end he would have what he desired. Is that truly honorable, when a man only acts because it is what he must do to have what he wants?"

Her brows scrunched together and her lips puckered into a frown. "I don't know. I guess it depends on what he does to get what he wants," she replied.

Daniel took her face in his hands, tilting her face upward so that she must look into his eyes when he spoke.

"I made a vow to Wicawa Ni Tu that I would give him the life of a Time Walker in exchange for peace," he said, his voice hoarse. "A *woman* Time Walker. I told him I would find his prisoner's woman. I told him I would bring *you* to him. It was what he asked in exchange for peace, and I did not care that I promised him a woman's life because of what I gained in return."

Her hands slid upward and around his neck, holding onto him as she raised her chin and met his stare.

"I know. I know what you promised him," she whispered. "And I know you better than that. You didn't know me when you made that promise. I know you did what you thought was best to avoid bloodshed that day. Do you think I believe anything else?"

"I see your trust in me. I will never let harm come to you. But there will be a time when I must decide again how to get what I want, and I tell you now that I will make that same choice. If it is the life of another forfeited so that I can keep you, then I will see it done."

"Daniel, I would never ask that of you –"

"It is not your choice to make," he replied.

He loosened his hold on her and let her go, stepping away. The echo of shouts from the village breached the silence and ricocheted through the cold air, and he recognized the call of his cousin among them before he saw Ahi Kekeleksu striding across the courtyard towards them.

"The prisoner escaped," Keke said when he reached their side. The warrior's hair was tied and knotted, and Daniel noted the freshly shorn half-moon scalp above his right ear. On Keke's back was the Norse sword gifted to him by their kinsmen when he became a man, secured by a crossed leather harness over his tunic.

"How long do we have?" Daniel asked.

Keke pulled the bow and quiver from his shoulder and thrust it into Emmy's hands. "Perhaps an hour. Maybe two," he said, his gaze fixed on Emmy. "You are a good shot. We will need you."

Emmy's mouth dropped open and she looked at Daniel.

"Wait. What are you doing? We're leaving *now*?" she asked, quite flustered as she shrugged the quiver over one shoulder and across her body.

Daniel looked at Keke, who was clearly ready to leave. Daniel had already told Keke of what he overheard Wicawa Ni Tu say that day in the woods near Emmy's cottage, and they both knew that they must go. If the Ricahecrians could not find Daniel or the Time Walker, then they would seek prey most easily found – that of Daniel and Keke's family at Basse's Choice.

"I sent a messenger ahead when we first arrived to warn them," Keke said.

"Warn who?" Emmy asked.

It was not how he meant to give it to her, but with the knowledge of what was to come, he had no choice. Daniel bent and unsheathed the knife from his boot, handing it to Emmy.

"Our family. Because they cannot find us, the Ricahecrians will go to Basse's Choice. They know my family lives there, and they will not stop until Wicawa Ni Tu finds a Time Walker."

He could see her hands were shaking when she saw what weapon he gave her. She ran her fingertips over the runes carved into the handle, and she pressed her thumb upon the Bloodstone on the hilt. A change came over her then and she raised her eyes, meeting his steady gaze. She knew it once belonged to her brother, and she knew what it meant.

"Then we need to leave," Emmy replied. Her voice rang with the realization of duty, clear and suddenly more resilient than he had ever witnessed from her lips. She closed her small hand tightly over the weapon and tucked it into her belt at her side.

Daniel wanted to take her into his arms, yet in the span of a few moments she had become something more to him. She would persevere through it all, and if he coddled her or tried to shelter her, she would crumble. As he looked into the depths of her jade eyes, he saw the gleam of a warrior in her stare. *No*, she is not a woman who will stand behind me, he thought. *She will stand beside me – and I will be glad for it.*

"Stay near me when the time comes," he said to her. "We are strongest when we are together."

He held out his hand. Emmy placed hers on his outstretched palm. Keke grunted something coarse in Paspahegh and followed suit, crushing them both when he squeezed their hands.

"I am ready to go home," Keke said.

"And we will," Daniel replied.

EMMY WAS RIGHT about Connor's condition. By the time they gathered their belongings and supplies and headed out towards Basse's Choice, Connor could not move his left arm or shoulder. He could move his right arm and only then he accomplished it with great difficulty. The paralytic effects of the stagger grass had set into the wound and spread, locking the muscles of his chest so that it took effort to breathe. It would not be long before his lower limbs were useless as well.

They took turns carrying the travois, rotating from sharing the task between two of them to having one person simply drag it. Emmy insisted on doing her fair share, and throughout the day as Daniel watched her, he could see exactly how she had dragged him back to her cottage without help. He wondered what it might have been like to know her brother better, or to understand how they had lived together in their future time. By whatever means Connor had trained his sister, he had pushed her to become a woman of substance. There was no doubt Connor succeeded in preparing her for her duties.

They did not stop to rest for hours. Daniel hoped they might barter for a canoe at the Weanock village near Charles City, but they had none to spare so they used their limited resources to secure passage across the James River. Travel by boat downstream would have reduced their time considerably, and although it would have been better for them all, he did not want to risk spending the time without movement. Basse's Choice was a day's trip by foot when walking at a brisk pace. The travois added time to their journey, and it was not long before Daniel realized they would not make it before nightfall.

The chilling scream of wars cries shattered the silence, echoing off the trees like the wail of spirits condemned to death. Emmy looked to him, her eyes wide, and she slipped her bow into ready position.

Keke lowered his end of the travois to the ground. Daniel met his cousin's dark eyes and he could read the resolution on his face. In all the years of his life, Ahi Kekeleksu had been by his side, urging Daniel to ignore the demons that taunted him for his mixed blood. It was Keke who told Daniel he was being a fool when Daniel spoke harsh words to their Uncle Winn and left home, and it was Keke who had made the journey to retrieve him from the Falls, even if it meant that he would only be bringing Daniel's body home for their uncle. Daniel could ask for no better man to stand by his side.

The black tipped feather entwined in Keke's hair twisted in the easy breeze off the river that came before dusk. He looked up at the sky as if he searched for guidance, his jaw firm and defiant in his resolve.

"I am tired of running, cousin," he said, lowering his head. Daniel widened his stance, planting his legs slightly apart. He took the bow from his shoulder and held it in one hand, placing the palm of his other hand on the butt of the knife at his waist.

"As am I," Daniel replied. "I feel the weight of their stares on my back, and I am weary of it." *Yes, he felt the enemy near.* He knew they were close even before he heard their war cries from that awareness of something down deep in his bones that told him why the sounds of the earth had silenced. It was the shadow of war and the heaviness of hatred that smothered them like water filling the lungs of a drowning man, and he could neither run from it nor allow it to taunt him any longer.

They would not make it to Basse's Choice in time. The Ricahecrians would not stop – and it was time to face them.

They placed their belongings in a pile near the tree line next to the place where the travois rested. Connor was still conscious, yet Daniel was sure he was aware of what was happening when he raised his head and spoke to Emmy, who kneeled at his side.

"Here, take this. There's one bullet left," she said. She removed the gun from her belt and placed it in Connor's hands, even twisting his finger around the trigger in readiness.

Daniel watched the exchange in silence, but the message from Connor's tenacious stare conveyed all he needed to know.

It was time.

Emmy drew her bow and stood beside him, while Keke flanked his other side with his sword ready. Daniel glanced at the sky and briefly closed his eyes, sending a prayer to the Gods of all men. Was it the Christian God he should pray to, or should he ask the Great Creator to smile upon them? He had never much considered what way was best before that moment, as if all the Gods that his kinsmen worshiped were always equal in his mind.

They came from the trees, one by one, stepping out around them in a circle as if they simply were born of the earth and merely there to confirm it. It no longer grieved him to consider these First People and wish for some way to make peace. He was a different man than the one that faced death at the Falls. Then, he was only a messenger, playing his part to make some sense of what his life should mean. Standing next to his cousin and the woman that would bear his sons, however, he was inflamed. There was much more at stake when he had something to lose other than his life.

Wicawa Ni Tu stepped forward. His eye bulged from the socket where scar tissue pulled at his face, but on his lips was the hint of a harsh grin. Despite the cold, the man was bare-chested, with paint streaked across his skin and a deerskin hanging loosely from his shoulders.

Daniel unsheathed the long-handled ax from his back that Cockacoeske had given him as a gift. It had once belonged to her father, and he considered it with great reverence. It was strange to him that the weapon of a Great Weroance would grace the hand of a half-blood such as himself, yet surely the Great Creator would guide his hand and help him use the sacred weapon.

"You should have died at the Falls for your treachery," Wicawa Ni Tu called out. Daniel walked forward a few paces to face the man, keeping a barrier between him and those he loved.

"Yes. Your warriors made a mistake by leaving me while there was still breath in my body," Daniel replied.

One of the warriors behind the War Chief snickered, and Wicawa Ni Tu scowled, snapping a quick utterance back at his men in a guttural growl.

"Perhaps. Yet now it is time to finish this. I see you have the woman," the War Chief said. When the warrior raised his chin and made to look behind Daniel, it sent a rush of fury straight through Daniel's chest.

"The woman is not part of this bargain," Daniel said. "I will return your captive to you. He will show you the way to use the magic, if you agree to let us leave in peace."

The moment the words left his lips he heard Emmy gasp. He turned back to her and saw that Keke had a firm grip on her arms, preventing her from leaving her spot. Daniel avoided her stare and went to Connor, who was already trying to get up off the travois. Connor was too weak to push himself up, but once Daniel supported him, he was able to stand. Connor shuffled towards Wicawa Ni Tu.

"No! No, I don't agree!" Emmy shouted. "Conner, no!"

At Emmy's outburst Connor paused and looked back. His right hand hung limply at his side, clutching the gun that Emmy had given him. He stared directly at her as he raised it, his hand shaking as he pointed it towards the trees. He pulled the trigger, releasing the last round, and Emmy let out a low moan when Connor dropped the gun into the dirt.

"Please, Daniel. Please, no," she begged him. Tears streamed down her face as the warriors brought Connor to the War Chief. They pushed him down on his knees and held him there, awaiting the command of their leader.

"I accept this gift," Wicawa Ni Tu announced. He turned his attention to Connor, grabbing him by his hair to lift his face. "Tell me now, Time Walker. How will your blood save my people? Tell me the secret of your magic."

Sweat poured down Connor's face and his hair stuck to his grey-tinged skin. His mouth moved and Daniel could not hear the words, but when Wicawa Ni Tu shook him brutally by the hair, Connor raised his voice.

"You must choose one person you wish to save," Connor ground out. He closed his eyes for a long moment before he opened them and spoke again, and all of those in the clearing seemed to lean in closer to hear him. "You can save one who is dead or dying if you use all of my lifeblood. I can only exchange my life for another. I cannot heal them all."

Behind him, Daniel could hear Emmy sobbing softly. Wicawa Ni Tu dropped Connor's head, seeming to consider his words.

"Is this true, Daniel Neilsson?" he asked.

Daniel nodded. "Yes. It is the way of the magic. A Blooded One may give life to the dead or heal the sick, but only by the gift of his own life." He said the words but they felt like poison on his lips. He did not wish to go along with Connor's plan yet there was no other choice. It was the only way to save Emmy, and it gave Connor the power of knowing he was giving his life for something greater than himself. Daniel understood that need better than any man, and when his sister's husband asked it of him, he gave him his word.

"This is what we will do," Connor said. *"I want you to return me to Wicawa Ni Tu. Tell him I will share the secret of how to use my blood, if he agrees to let you go on your way."*

Daniel immediately drew back, dropping Connor's hand.

"We can take you to Basse's Choice – the blood of a newborn will heal you. There is no need to think of this. We will take you there and you will be healed – and then you will share this journey with your sister and me," *Daniel replied.*

Connor shook his head, a bitter grin on his face. "You mean the child of your cousin, Dagr Neilsson? His wife does not give birth for two more weeks. I looked in the book, the family bloodline trees are there. I'm not making it through this, Daniel. You need to help me do this. For Emmy. So at least it means something when I die."

Connor thrust his hand out and grasped Daniel's arm once more. Daniel gripped him in return, and it was decided.

Perhaps it was self-serving when he agreed to it, yet Daniel knew he would make the same decision again if given the chance. There was only harsh reality before them, and there was nothing any of them could do to save Connor. Given a choice between assisting a dying man to a speedy death or sending Emmy to certain slaughter, he would choose the man each time and never dwell on it.

Wicawa Ni Tu issued an order to his men, and one of them pulled back Connor's head and thrust a knife under his chin.

"I fear you tell me what I already know," the War Chief said. He looked past Daniel, pointing his spear at Emmy. "Yet I have heard stories that the children of Time Walkers are even more powerful. I have heard tales that say every child from your womb will have this power, and that they can heal many people until the day the child no longer drinks from your breast."

"That's not true!" Connor shouted hoarsely. Wicawa Ni Tu's head snapped back to Connor.

"Oh, yes, I think it is. That is why you think you can fool me. Why should I have a dying Time Walker, when I can wed the Time Walker woman and make many more?"

Connor lunged at Wicawa Ni Tu. The man holding the knife raked the blade across Connor's throat, slicing cleanly through his throat. Chaos erupted as the blood spilled onto the earth and Connor dropped to the ground, shuddering in his death throes as his life drained away.

Emmy elbowed Keke in the belly and twisted away from him, getting off one shot with her bow before the warriors attacked. She felled one rushing man, causing the others to reconsider and fall back. Daniel was sure that they intended to bring her to their Chief unharmed, so they at least had that in their favor.

Daniel swung all his might into the blow of his long-handled ax, sending a Ricahecrian to the ground. Keke thrust his sword into the belly of a man who came too close, kicking the man out of the way as he pulled the blade from the body. Daniel and Emmy put their backs to Keke, and they faced the circle of warriors that slowly advanced on them.

"Ten left by my count," Keke said. Daniel cocked his head, shouldering up to his cousin.

"Five for you and five for me," he muttered in reply.

"I can shoot at least three more before they reach us," Emmy hissed. Daniel darted a glance at her, grateful that she held back. He could see her lower lip trembling but her hand was steady, poised with one arrow ready to fly.

Wicawa Ni Tu stepped forward, holding his arms out wide to his sides. Daniel felt Emmy flinch when the man rested his foot on Connor's body, propping his knee up as he called out to them.

210

"Give me the woman and I will let you live," the War Chief shouted.

Before Daniel could answer, another voice from behind them roared a response.

"Run now, and perhaps we will not kill you all!" Winn Neilsson bellowed.

Daniel felt Emmy fall against him as Winn ran past them with at least a dozen other men in his wake. He had never seen his uncle fight, nor witnessed the image of such raw power in one place. Winn wielded a sword as few men could do, slicing clear through the shoulder of the first man to challenge him. The others swarmed around them, leaving Daniel stunned for a moment before someone shoved him, and when he whipped around with his ax raised he was met by the half-gleeful smirk of his Uncle Erich.

"Think ye might want to help us, ye young brat?" he bellowed. His thick reddish blond hair was bound in war braids and it seemed the stout man had shaved his scalp in the style of his Norse kinsman for the occasion. "I may be old, but I'm not dead yet. It's been some time since I've had the stain of blood on this blade, but not so long I've forgotten how to stand beside my kin. Hurry now, it appears we have a few men to cut down!"

Erich raised his sword and rushed forward, screaming insults at their enemy that would chill the blood of any man.

Daniel nodded, quite speechless until Emmy jabbed him in the ribs.

"Who was that?" she demanded. She let loose a flurry of arrows, glancing sideways at him in wait for his answer.

"My family," he said simply.

His vision was suddenly clear. He joined his kinsmen in battle, pushing back the Ricahecrians until there were few left who did not flee. Emmy stayed by his side, firing arrows at retreating men until she had no more, and even then she threw down her bow and took up her knife.

Daniel took a blow to his side with a club before he swung around and brought his ax down on the warrior's head, splitting him with a sickening crunch and spew of blood to bring him to the ground. Daniel fell down on one knee from the momentum, bowing his head and gasping to recover his wind.

As he slowly rose to his feet and raised his eyes, he gladly met the man who stood waiting in his path. Wicawa Ni Tu stood there, bloodied and unwavering, holding his arms out to Daniel in challenge.

Daniel knew all the other Ricahecrians were dead, and that his kinsmen now surrounded them in wait. They would not advance unless Daniel told them to do so, yet he knew that he would not ask it of them because it was a battle he must face alone.

"Come, little warrior," Wicawa Ni Tu taunted him, waving his fingers in welcome. Daniel repositioned the ax in his hands, feeling his grip mesh into the handle despite the slippery blood on his skin.

They crashed together in a tangle of limbs, each trying to gain the advantage. Wicawa Ni Tu was strong and lean, but Daniel was larger and quicker. Be it pure willpower or sheer fury, it was not long before Daniel took him to the ground, the knuckles of his fists raw and bloodied as he hit the man again and again.

Through a broken nose and shattered teeth, Wicawa Ni Tu smiled up at Daniel.

"I bathed in the blood of the Pamunkey, and then I let the ravens peck out the eyes of the dead," Wicawa Ni Tu spat. "They will never find the afterlife without their eyes to guide them."

Daniel straightened his back and stood up, swinging the ax wide before he brought it down on the warrior's head, splitting it like a ripe melon.

"Neither will you," Daniel replied. He went down on one knee, looking at the body of his enemy, and despite the hate in his heart, he asked the Great Creator to show his spirit the way home.

It was all he could do for those he never wished to kill, and for what was left of his soul when he turned to face his family.

15

Emmy

HER ENTIRE BODY felt numb when they arrived at Basse's Choice. She rode the entire way in silence, sitting behind Daniel on the back of a horse. Keke rode at their side, dragging the travois with Connor's body behind his mount. The yellow glow of moonlight was high over the earth when she slipped off the horse and let Daniel lead her inside a house, and despite the women and children bustling around them, Emmy heard very little of what they said.

Someone cleaned her face with a rough rag, but it was warm and she closed her eyes and let them have their way. She did not particularly care if there was the blood of their enemies was on her face, nor did she care if it stayed there. It was part of her now, just as Connor had once been part of her, and for all the days of her life she would never forget how it felt to take a man's life – or to see a man she loved die.

She felt the bench beneath her bottom and gripped it with her fingertips. The wood was quite soft, allowing enough give so that she could dig her fingernails into the grain. *There*, she thought. *That was something. I think a splinter is jammed under my nail.*

"Cat got your tongue?" someone asked. It was a woman's voice and it was different from the others. There was no thick accent, like the man called Erich, nor was it precise and careful as Daniel's uncle Winn spoke. She suspected she was losing her mind and that it was sheer shock that caused her to think it was an American, but she opened her eyes anyway and tried to focus on the woman in front of her.

"No. I can talk just fine," Emmy whispered in reply. The woman smiled, her gentle green eyes visibly softened in relief. Her hair was long and red, curling up at the ends and around her face. The only signs of her age were the tiny lines around her eyes that crinkled when she smiled, but if not for that one might mistake her for a much younger woman.

"Well, that's good. I didn't think anyone cut out your tongue, but you never know around here," the woman muttered with a smile. "I'm Maggie, Daniel's aunt. Are you okay?"

Emmy nodded. "I think so," she said softly. No, she was not okay, but if she admitted it out loud she feared she might start screaming, and judging from the room full of children she figured that would be the wrong thing to do at that moment.

"Are those Gap jeans? I never thought I'd see any of those things again. Well, I'm afraid they're too damaged to save, but if you want to wear pants I'll have some mended to fit you," Maggie said. Emmy stared at the woman, aware that her mouth gaped slightly open.

"You're – you're from my time?" Emmy sputtered.

"I left in 2012, so I'm guessing you weren't far off?"

"I – I – I'm from 2014," she replied. "Daniel said you were like me, but I didn't think ... I mean, I had no idea *when* you were from."

"My family is quite full of those who are like you. How old are you?" Maggie asked, wringing out the bloody rag in a bucket of water.

"Twenty-two," she said. Maggie nodded, as if to herself, and smiled.

"Daniel's only a year older than you. It will be a good match."

Emmy clamped her mouth shut at that declaration. The reality of her situation rushed back in one fell swoop. She needed to get a hold of herself, and she needed to talk to Daniel.

A young girl with long curly black hair rushed by and Maggie snatched her by the belt of her dress and pulled her onto her lap. The girl squirmed when Maggie kissed her cheek, her cheeks dimpling at both sides when her lips split into a wide grin.

"Aw, gramma!" the girl whined, wiped the kiss from her cheek.

"Oh, shush, Finola," Maggie admonished her. "I want you to meet this nice lady. Finola, this is Miss Emmy."

Finola dipped her head politely in Emmy's direction.

"Pleased to meet you, Miss Emmy," the child said. "Can I go now? Daniel promised me a piggy-back ride before I go back to bed."

"Shoo then, silly pants," Maggie replied, letting the child jump off her lap. "That's my daughter Kyra's youngest. She just turned seven last week. She's a Blooded One, but don't mention it to her mother. Kyra doesn't want anything to do with all that business since she's a sworn Christian now. I have another grandchild due any time now, as soon as Dagr's wife decides she's ready, of course."

"Oh, of course," Emmy replied. *So even if they had reached Basse's Choice, Connor could not have been saved*, Emmy thought. Had her brother known that when he made his plan, or was it just chance?

She kept watch on the child as she raced through the house and waited patiently for the door to open, leaping at Daniel the moment he came through the door. He was immediately surrounded by the children and he picked Finola up and continued to greet them all, taking the hearty embraces as he balanced Finola on his hip. Despite the throng of people that surrounded him, his eyes met hers across the room, the weight of his stare seeming to ask a question she did not yet know how to answer.

She lowered her gaze. Maggie made a short snorting sound.

"It's like that, is it?" Maggie commented.

"I don't know what you mean."

"He'll come to you, and you'll mend things. The men in this family never can stand it when a woman's displeased with him."

"I'm not angry at him," Emmy said softly. She didn't actually know what she felt because the grief was too fresh for her to consider anything else.

"Well, good. Because he's coming over here and you're going to need to talk to him."

Maggie stood up abruptly and threw her arms around Daniel's neck, squeezing him tightly. He hugged her in return and let her kiss his cheeks, a chagrined half-smile on his face and his skin flushing at the attention.

"You're impossible, you know that?" she chastised him. "Winn and I were worried sick about you!" He issued her a boyish grin, shaking his head in denial.

"I surely learned it from my aunt," he replied. Daniel placed his hand in his pocket and fumbled for a moment, then pulled out something in his closed fist which he held out to Maggie.

"Oh, my," Maggie said when Daniel opened his hand. Lying on his outstretched palm was a gold timepiece with a fine gold chain attached to it rolled up in his palm. He handed it to Maggie, who seemed speechless.

"I thought it might soften your heart, Aunt," he said quietly. "Or that you might forgive me for the harsh words spoken between us when I left."

Maggie's face flushed bright pink with the effort of holding back her tears. She clutched the timepiece in her hand and nodded.

"You didn't need to bring me a gift. Your safe return is all the blessing I need," she replied. Emmy smiled when they hugged, glad that Daniel had mended things with the women who had raised him.

"Daniel, why don't you show Emmy to your room? You can bunk with the men in the barn loft since it looks like they're all staying," Maggie suggested, wiping tears from her eyes with the edge of her sleeve.

"I will, thank you," he said. He held his hand out to her and Emmy slowly grasped it, letting him guide her to the back of the house where a narrow hallway led to a door.

The chaos of the homecoming dimmed to a distant chatter, and once they entered the back room and Daniel closed the door she welcomed the silence. It was a small room with only a few furnishings, with a narrow cot and a trunk in the corner.

As she sat down on the bed, Daniel removed her backpack from his shoulder. He set it beside her and took out the book, opening it up and scrolling through it. He paused when he came to a page that was made of thick parchment, and he opened the flap to retrieve the letter he handed to her. It was sealed with wax and it looked like someone had pressed their thumb into it in lieu of a stamp. She traced the lines of the thumbprint lightly with her fingertip.

On the outside of the folded paper was a short sentence, written in block print.

Emmy - Read this when you arrive at Basse's Choice in 1656.

"He asked me to see that you read the letter," Daniel said softly. She knew *who* she meant. Of course Connor had asked it of Daniel, as if she had expected that anything less than the fact that Connor had managed to arrange his own death in the way he saw fit. She could see in Daniel's face that he thought she blamed him, but she could not find the words to convey what was truly running through her mind.

They stood beside each other and killed people that day, she thought. *She shot men with her arrows as if they were animals, as if it meant nothing. Daniel was alive, and so was she. Yet Connor was dead, and there was no bringing him back this time.*

When Daniel turned to go, she reached for him, taking his hand before he could leave her.

"Will you stay with me while I read it?" she asked. She didn't know what to expect or what the letter might mean to her, but with everything that had happened that day she knew she wanted him with her to face it. He sat down beside her on the bed, returning the book to her backpack on the floor.

The red wax seal stayed intact when it popped off the brittle paper and she set it aside in her lap while she started to read.

Dear Emelia Leigh,

I hope this letter finds you well. If you've followed the directions and waited until the right time to read this, then I expect that you've already made it through the winter. I know it has been difficult and sometimes you wanted to give up, but believe me – you're on the right track.

Please do not be angry at Connor. We all have a place in this world and we all must play our part in the timeline. His timeline was meant to end, just as yours is meant to go on.

If you do manage to manipulate things and change the past, be assured that time will find a way to right itself. You cannot change the past without consequence, and sometimes the way things are fixed is much more difficult to bear than what was supposed to happen in the first place. There is a reason the Five Northmen and the Five Chiefs made a blood vow to protect the Blooded Ones. I'm sure you understand that right now. Can you imagine what life you might have led as Wicawa Ni Tu's wife? There are generations of

Blooded Ones who lived their lives in servitude as nothing more than broodmares to men like him. Mourn Connor for what he did, but know that he did it out of love and devotion to you and the children you will someday have.

As for Daniel, well, what can I say that you don't already know? Of course it was difficult to trust him in the beginning, that's how you were raised. His place in your life, however, is not negotiable. Don't be too hard on him. There is no place in time where you could have found a better match, or found a man who would give his life just to see you happy and safe.

By now you must have realized that Smithfield is a part Basse's Choice. It won't be called Smithfield until after 1725, and your family will live there for a long time.

What matters now, however, is that you travel with Daniel to Middle Plantation, the future site of Williamsburg. When you arrive at Middle Plantation, you need to find a man named Torquil Campbell and he will be expecting you. He might find you first, but if you need to go looking, you'll find him either at the town ordinary or at the Cooper's shop near the docks. You'll know him when you see him, he has a way of standing out in a crowd.

I'm pretty much breaking the rules by writing this letter. I figure I'm not changing anything or telling you anything you don't already know, but I can't shake this odd feeling that something could go wrong. I know how you get sometimes, so I'm going to give you a little push in the right direction.

I guess that's about it. Daniel offered to write this for me, but I figured I had a better chance of getting you to listen if I wrote it myself. And no, before you go off half-cocked over thinking this is just a forgery, remember the time you stole your father's Bloodstone dagger that your mother kept in the back of her closet in a shoe box, and Connor and your mother tore the house apart looking for it? Well, they never found it, and eventually you gave up out of sheer guilt. You pried up the ...

"The third floorboard from the north corner," Emmy whispered, clutching the paper in complete disbelief. Daniel raised a brow but said nothing, waiting for her to speak.

There was one person in the world who knew that spot, but reading the words from her own hand was something immensely terrifying and exhilarating at the same time. She blinked her eyes and continued reading.

... third floorboard from the north corner in your bedroom and retrieved it. That should be sufficient to prove I am who I say I am.

I can't give you any more advice. Just be where you're supposed to be, and make sure you don't drive Daniel nuts while you're getting there.

Happy Travels,

Emmy Neilsson (nee Cameron)

Emmy folded the letter closed. She picked up the wax seal and pressed her thumb upon it, not surprised when it was a perfect match.

"Emmy Neilsson," she whispered. *So she had satisfied the first part of her journey – and Daniel would accompany her on the rest of it.* She found some measure of solace in the fact that she had completed that task, yet the remainder of the unknown still weighed heavy on her heart.

She placed the letter in her backpack and turned to Daniel's curious gaze. It was clear he had questions, just as surely as she did, but she knew with every bone in her body that they would discover those truths together.

"I will leave you to your thoughts. If you need me, I will not be far," he said, standing up.

"Will you stay with me tonight?" she asked. She would worry on seventeenth-century propriety later. For the moment, she needed his strength, and tomorrow they could deal with reality.

"Of course," he said. They undressed by the glimmer of the candlelight and settled down together on the narrow cot.

He slipped into the bed beside her and pulled her to him, cradling her tightly against him. She curled against him like a bow, fitting perfectly, content to rest in the wake of his embrace. His breathing had eased to a slow rhythm and she thought he was asleep when he finally spoke, his words whispered in the dim flicker of light and brushing against her cheek like a brand upon her skin.

"Will you forgive me?" he asked. She squeezed her eyes tightly closed, refusing to let the tears surface.

"There is nothing to forgive," she said softly. She meant it. She knew it was Connor's decision, and she knew that Daniel had tried to tell her before they left the Pamunkey village. "I wanted to save him, but I understand. He must have known he was not meant to live. It was what he needed to do to know that he made a difference. I *know* why he did it."

"But my part in it –"

"I forgive you. I forgave you the moment it happened. I know why you did it. And I would do the same for you," she said. "I would do the same to keep you."

His lips lowered onto hers, seeking and searching as if he meant to claim her all over once more. Yet she already belonged to him. The thing between them loomed greater than the pull of time or duty, crushing what was left of what they once believed true.

She burrowed into him, burying her face into his arm while he clutched her hips against his.

"I will keep the light burning," he whispered as she was close to falling asleep, "so you need not fear the darkness." She nodded and relaxed into his embrace, letting the welcome nothingness of sleep take her away.

16

Daniel

DANIEL TIGHTENED THE leather strap that secured the traveling pack to the saddle, ensuring that the weight was comfortable for the horse to carry. He was grateful that his uncle had two horses to spare, and although Winn called them a wedding gift, Daniel knew the animals were a precious commodity. The animal snorted and stomped his hoof with the last yank, and Daniel patted the horse's neck in apology.

The promise of springtime was upon the land, bringing the trees to blossom and bloom. It was mild that morning with a hint of warmth in the air, and with the golden amber sunshine rising in the east and the damp soil beneath his feet, Daniel suspected they would have a pleasant journey to Middle Plantation. Emmy was a skilled rider, so he had no doubt she would handle the trek without difficulty.

"Easy," he murmured, scratching the horse along his thick black mane. The animal shook his head and uttered a low whinny, and when Daniel spotted Winn walking across the courtyard towards him, he understood why.

"Here," Winn said, thrusting a handful of corncobs at Daniel. "Your aunt is fond of this old beast, so take good care of him. He comes from good stock. I am sure he will serve you well."

"Thank you," Daniel replied. He let the horse take a nip of corn and put the rest in the saddle pack.

"She does not wish you to go," Winn said. It was unlike his uncle to make idle conversation, so when he brought up Aunt Maggie, Daniel knew Winn likely had the same reservations his wife did.

"I know. But it is not her that lives in my skin, and she does not understand that I am ready to go," Daniel replied. He swallowed hard, trying to find the right words to make Winn understand. "Emmy has a duty to fulfill, and I must stand beside her to see it through. There is no place I would rather spend my days than by her side."

Winn made a low snorting sound, crossing his arms over his chest. His lips were set in a thin line and his blue eyes squinted at Daniel, as if he thought him addled.

"I know what it means to carry the burden of duty, son," Winn said. "Yet I do not think it means you must run towards your own end."

Daniel softened at the term of endearment. Winn had raised him as his own, and he had never treated Daniel as anything other than his son. It was the reason he respected and loved him, and it was why he wanted to be the kind of son Winn might be proud of.

"If there is another way, I will find it," Daniel replied. "I will keep trying, until I have no other choice. I promise you that."

Winn nodded. The worry on his dark chiseled face was clear, yet there was a sad acceptance there as well.

His braid of black hair fell over his shoulder as he placed a hand upon the horse's mane and looked at the beast, patting it firmly on the neck.

"Your father asked me once why I did not kill Maggie when I first found her," Winn said. "She was a Time Walker, and I was sworn to take her head to our uncle, the Great Weroance Opechancanough. Makedewa said he would do it for me, if I was so weak that I could not kill one useless white woman."

Daniel was surprised to see Winn smile and shake his head. He knew the story of how his uncle met his aunt, but he had never heard what his own father, Makedewa, thought of it.

"My brother hated Maggie for a long time. He blamed her for our exile from the Paspahegh, and for the magic in her veins that brought Opechancanough's ire upon us. Then we went to battle in the Great Assault of '22."

"How did you recover from that destruction?" Daniel asked, the words spilling forth. Winn met his gaze.

"The same as you will, for what you saw at the Falls. The same as Makedewa did, when he saved your mother," Winn replied. "Once he met your mother, his vision changed. It was only then that he understood why I could not kill Maggie, even if prophecy or duty compelled me to do so. He knew then what it was to leave your heart in the keeping of another."

Daniel nodded. "I know what that is like," he admitted.

"I know that you do. Yet you are much like your father, and I fear for what will happen as you walk this path. I cannot make you stay, but I ask you to return to us someday if you can. Both of you, return to us."

"I will," Daniel promised. He embraced the only father he had ever known, which was a rare thing for the men of his family to do except when saying goodbye. To him it was a promise, a vow he intended to keep.

"John Basse is here!" Aunt Maggie called out. She looked at them in a peculiar manner as the men broke apart, the hint of a sad smile on her face.

"Won't you at least stay the night? You can't rightly spend your wedding night in a strange place," Maggie grumbled, hooking her arm through Winn's elbow.

"Emmy and I both agree, we will leave after the ceremony," Daniel replied.

"I tried to reason with him, wife. Leave him be, he has made up his mind," Winn intoned, kissing Maggie lightly on her forehead. "Good travels, Daniel," he said. Daniel and Winn clasped hands, and Winn left them to help John Basse settle in.

"You can still change your mind. You don't even know what you'll find at Middle Plantation! What if it's something dangerous? If it hasn't happened yet, it can be changed. It's not too late to –"

"You who raised me, mother of my heart," Daniel interrupted. "Surely you of all people understand why I must go. I have been between two worlds for all my years, yet now, with her, I know where my future lies, and even if it is my end, I want it – with her. 'Tis with her, by her side, and we will finish this task; I will spend my last breath to see this through. There is no tomorrow for me but the one I share with her. We will travel to Middle Plantation and fulfill her task, and I will not leave her side until we see it finished."

Maggie placed her palms on his cheeks, looking up into his eyes. She smiled then, the best smile he imagined she could under the circumstances, and she kissed his cheek.

"Well, I suppose there's no changing your mind, then," she said softly, her throat contracting and her eyes slightly reddened. "Just be safe. Be happy, and be safe. And know that we will always be here waiting for you."

He picked her up and hugged her, noticing for the first time in his life just how small his aunt was. She smacked him lightly on the arm and marched off to see the minister, yanking her dress back into place as she walked away.

Daniel leaned against the horse and silently watched the bustle in the courtyard for his wedding. *He was blessed beyond measure – and he would do everything he could to keep all the blessings he had.*

THEIR WEDDING WAS a simple affair, attended by his family at Basse's Choice, and they left as soon as it was over. Although neither of them needed a ceremony, it was important to Daniel that they were bound by English law before they started their journey together. Middle Plantation was not far by horseback, but once they arrived there was no way to predict what they would face.

He guided his mount up the gentle grassy slope, stopping at the peak overlooking a meadow. It had been a long time since he visited the place, save for Connor's burial, and it still seemed strange to him at the time that it was where his mother and father rested. He recalled climbing the hill as a young boy, eager to sit by the graves and find some solace, or find some sense in a world that seemed neither to belong to him or need him. The burial mounds gave no answer, however, and when he became a man his visits became less frequent. The living had no answers for him, so why would the dead serve to guide him?

The horse snorted and stomped in protest when Daniel dismounted, but the beast took the opportunity to grab a mouthful of grass while he was loose.

"Thank you for letting me say goodbye," Emmy said. Daniel helped her down off her horse. Although she did not need the assistance, she smiled when he placed his hands on her waist and lowered her to the ground.

"I thought you might like to come here before we go. I do not know when we will return," he replied. *Or if we will return*, he thought. He would not share that sentiment with her, however. He had a new vision of what was to come and he was determined to find a way.

Connor's fresh grave was covered with a blanket of dried flowers, aged in the time since they had buried him. He took Emmy's hand as she looked down upon it and she gave him a reassuring squeeze in return.

"Did you come here often? I mean, before we buried Connor?" she asked. She tilted her chin upwards, her hair brushed back off her face from the wisp of wind swirling on the hilltop.

The graves of his father and mother were barren, reduced to shallow unmarked mounds. The earth had a way of doing that, taking back what belonged to it, and Daniel knew that it would not be very long before no one remembered the graves upon that hill.

"Yes. When I was a boy, I did," he admitted. "And after I read the book and knew my fate, I asked my uncle to see that I was buried here."

His wife's hand tightened in his. He smiled, loving her defiance. It was what he needed from her, and the only way they would conquer what was to come.

Daniel slipped his hand down over Emmy's gently rounded belly. He wondered what their son would look like, and he longed for the day he might hold him in his arms. "It will be many years before we must think of where to lay our bones," he said. "I promise you that, *eholen.*" He was through with letting predictions of the future control him, and he was ready to find a way to change it.

"I know," she said, kissing him gently on his lips. "Because I won't let you leave this earth without me."

Daniel helped his wife onto her horse and mounted up. He did not turn back when they left, keeping his eyes on the path ahead. With a bit of luck, they would reach Middle Plantation by nightfall, and he had no doubt that it was where they were both meant to be.

We will have many tomorrows, he thought. *For I am not yet ready to leave this life.*

The End

Dear Reader,

Thank you for reading GHOST DANCE. The second volume in the series, SEASON OF EXILE, will be available in May 2017. If you enjoyed GHOST DANCE, please consider leaving a review on Amazon to share your experience with other readers. Thank you!

Click HERE to be notified when SEASON OF EXILE is released

Enjoy a sneak peek at the series that started it all!

Preview: The Legend of the Bloodstone

(Time Walkers, Book 1)

CHAPTER 1

James County, Virginia

October 2012

"STUPID FREAKIN' BARN," she muttered.

There really was no good reason for her to be out in the old barn this late, but she would lose what was left of her composure if she sat in the empty house any longer. She could hear grandpa as if he stood there beside her, his accent slurring his words together as it did when he was angry.

"Maggie-Mae, yer head is full of bricks, I swear it, girl!"

Although she wanted to smile at the thought, she could not. It was still too fresh, too raw. Her lips twisted downward, and she shook off the flash of anger that surged as she thrust her fists into her front jean pockets and took a swipe at a tuft of loose straw with her boot.

Death sucked; there was nothing much more to say about it. No one to blame, no way for her to fight the advance of time. The Reaper claimed him, and there was not a blessed thing she could do about it.

Making things right around the farm? Well, there was a problem she could manage, and she had two good hands and two strong legs to work with. At least it was something.

Sunset dipped away beyond the horizon and the crimson orange sky streaked with that glowing time of peace before nightfall, her anger seeming like an intrusion into the cycle of nature. The wind kicked up, fluttering the edges of her red parka so she zipped it fully closed, putting off the luxury of mourning when there was so much work to do. She heard the roar of the waterfall beyond the meadow, the riverbanks swollen to overflowing from the recent storm. It left the ground saturated, like an overused sponge.

Her hood fell back off her head with the next gust of wind and the rain soaked her long hair as she walked through the courtyard back to the barn, the damp earth squishing beneath her boots.

The old dairy barn loomed first on her to-do list. Over one hundred years old, the field stone foundation stood crumbling in some spots, in dire need of reinforcement. Determined to ready it for the construction work, she labored to clear the debris most of the afternoon. It was a solitary task, one that kept her occupied until early evening, but she was pleased with her efforts and glad for the distraction. It would be quite useful as a private foaling box when it was finally finished, far enough from the main horse barn to provide a birthing sanctuary for the broodmares.

Maggie shook the stiff work gloves off her soiled hands and threw them onto the bale of musty straw at her feet. The muscles in her shoulders ached and her legs cramped at the effort, yet she bent to tighten the laces on her sodden work boots anyway. She rested one hand against the cold stone wall to balance herself, but as she rose up she noticed a few rocks cluttering the ground. She considered ignoring the debris, then felt foolish after she worked so hard all day. What difference would it make if she spent a few more minutes picking up rocks? She had nothing else to do anyway.

"Move yer lazy ass!" she berated herself. A laugh escaped her lips at the thought of how silly it was to be talking to no one in an empty barn, and she promptly bent to the task. She grasped the hem of her parka upward until it pouched, then tossed a few of the smaller stones into her makeshift bucket. As she reached out closer to the wall to chase a stone poking out beneath the scattered straw, something sharp jabbed her fingers and she drew back at the flash of pain.

"Damn it!" she muttered. She jerked her arm away and sat back on her heels, grasping her throbbing fingers with her other hand and trying to hold the rocks in her parka up with her elbow. A trickle of bright red blood dripped from two torn digits, both sliced clean across the fingertips. She instinctively raised them to her lips and stuck them in her mouth and her rock collection tumbled to the floor. It was a disgusting habit and probably not very sanitary, but it was the only thing to do at the time.

To her dismay, her questionable method did little to stem the bleeding. She swore a few words under her breath and kicked her boot across the straw to find the source of her injury. It would likely turn out to be a rusted nail or piece of metal, and she scowled when she figured her tetanus shot was most likely overdue.

"What addles yer brain, Maggie? I told you I would clear the barn!"

Fingers still clenched around her bleeding hand, she glanced up to see Marcus striding toward the barn. Twenty years her senior and adamant about a promise to her grandfather to watch over her, he took his oath seriously, watching for a chance to swoop in and honor his duty. His hulking shoulders braced against the rain, the moisture dappling his unruly swatch of black hair and dripping into rivulets down his tight jaw. She could see his thick brows furrow over the slit of his eyes as he approached, stomping through the mud and apparently oblivious to the slush he sent flying in his wake.

"*Me brain* is just fine, Marcus," she teased, mimicking his thick accent. His brows narrowed but his eyes twinkled as she rolled her eyes upward and gave him a half-hearted grin, holding up her damaged digits for his inspection. The wound to her fingers continued pulsing, obviously in need of a few stitches. "But my fingers have a little problem."

"Funny girl," he grumbled as he inspected her hand. "What on Earth! Did you need to work yerself bloody? Couldn't just listen to me for once and stay in the house, you red-headed hellion!" he snapped.

"I couldn't stay in there anymore, Marcus...I needed to be busy."

He blotted her bleeding hand with the edge of his flannel shirt, but raised his gaze to hers at her response. His faced creased and his eyes widened as she scrunched her nose and tried to shake off the glimmer of wetness threatening to spill from her eyes.

"Ah, I'm sorry," he grunted, dropping her hand and pulling her into a hug. "I didn't mean to shout at you. Your granddad would kick my arse for treating you so."

"I can kick your ass on my own," she sniffed, leaning her head against his shoulder for a moment. His chest rumbled and his arms tightened around her as he chuckled, and she could not resist a poorly aimed punch to his kidney.

"Maybe, my wee terror, maybe," he agreed. With one calloused hand, he smoothed her damp hair from her forehead and looked into her face. "But I miss him, too, you know, very much." His voice cracked with the words, and Maggie flinched at the uncommon emotion. Marcus had always been her constant, a steady guide throughout any crisis. The oldest friend of her grandfather and the closest thing to family she had, the solemn giant was all that was left to keep her grounded to a life that seemed more like a distant dream.

"Yeah, well, there's still work to do," she mumbled, uncomfortable at sharing her sadness lest she fall down a slope with no way to scramble out. She stepped away from him and wiped her hand on the leg of her denim jeans, avoiding his gaze to avert any more shared grief.

"Ah, there is, but you need a few stitches first. The mess will still be here on the morrow, I promise to leave it for you, but yer done for tonight. I'll bring the truck around, wait here out of the rain."

She said nothing but nodded, acquiescence easier when it remained silent. His mouth tightened in a thin line and he shook his head as he walked away, muttering under his breath. Maggie turned back to the pile of debris and bent to clear it before he returned.

She did not locate the source of her injury, but she found the last few rocks. She picked one up and meant to toss it in her makeshift pouch, but it felt warm as if it had laid in the sun all day and she paused to look closer at it. It was oval shaped and smooth against her palm, and in the glare of the single light bulb hanging above her head, it gleamed a dark green color, nearly black. Her hand throbbed again, but this time it was from the spreading warmth in her palm beneath the stone. She leaned one hand against the stone wall to steady herself as she looked closer at it and noticed there was a vein of crimson running through the center. Had she stained the stone with her own blood?

Bile suddenly rose in her throat and she choked back a wave of nausea. Shaking her head in disgust of her own weakness, she supposed the chore could wait until the morning and she could surely use the rest. She clutched the smooth rock in her bloody palm and pushed off the wall with her good hand to stand. Her vision abruptly exploded in a halo of darkness.

"Whoa," she said, reaching for the wall and missing. Tiny bursts of stars now filled the blackness, and she grabbed for the wall again without success. Was she going to pass out? She thought it might be best to sit down, but control of her traitorous body was lost. Her legs buckled and collapsed in a useless heap as the rest of her flaccid body followed.

"Maggie? *Maggie!*"

She heard the echo of his voice but could not respond, unable to push the words from her throat with the pressure of the darkness engulfing her. An urge to lie down on the ground pulled her closer to the floor, as if she could melt through the dirt and join somehow with some primal force to stop the maddening spin of her senses.

She felt a burning in her palm as the strange pulling sensation increased, reminded of that time as a child when she waded too far out in the ocean and the current became too strong. The riptide sucked her out, persistent at first, but quickly changed into a demanding dredge that pulled her further and further from shore. Her first impulse was to fight the pull, but as it began to rise the pressure was too great, and the only thing left was to submit and let it carry her away. Marcus was her savior that day, but in the barn, no one could help her. Now the power surged from the stinging in her hand and the tide heaved her down to the earth where she thought if she could only press her cheek to the damp ground, the urge might be relieved.

A sliver of fear washed through her blood as her vision began to change, the dark haze overcome by a growing ember of light. *Bright, it was so bright!* Her shoulder gave way and she let her head follow, eager now to make the pressure stop, but perplexed that the light now surged stronger, blinding her, with each inch she pressed closer to the earth. Numbness throbbed in every muscle, coursed throughout her limbs, and churned in a heap in her belly. It proceeded to drop down deep through her gut, and she thought she surely would vomit. She opened her eyes.

Only a shimmering sunset greeted her confusion, a sunset that seemed to grow larger and larger until it engulfed her. At last, when she thought she would burn because she could not tolerate the heat anymore, she dug her face into the cold mud and closed her eyes to the madness.

CHAPTER 2

SOMETHING TASTED GRITTY and damp when she tried to moisten her cracked lips. She figured she must have slept like a rock if she was waking up with a cottonmouth, but when she tried to swallow all she could taste was...dirt. Maggie sighed and rolled over, and when she opened her eyes, nothing made sense at all.

The palms of her hands were caked with wet earth when she pushed herself into a sitting position.

"What the hell?" she groaned. She blinked a few times in an effort to clear the sleep from her eyes, and when her gaze finally sharpened, she was dismayed to find she truly was sitting on the ground. It also appeared she had rolled around in the dirt, because as she held each arm extended away from her body she could see the mud slathered on her skin.

A crescent moon was shining overhead illuminating the evergreens in a silver glimmer, the sounds of a busy forest smothering her senses. She was sitting in a patch of damp earth in the middle of the woods. Her fingers dug into the earth as the heady scent of evergreen needles fell upon her, and she could still taste the bitter blood residue in her mouth from her wound.

Ok, she knew what was going on. She must be dreaming. It was the only explanation. *Time to wake up!* She closed her eyes again, knowing when she opened them she would be safe in her own bed, snug and cozy like she was supposed to be. Not sitting on her ass in the middle of the night in a forest.

She gave it a go. Eyes closed, she counted backward in a methodical manner from ten to one. Yup, that should do the trick!

Oh, good Lord Jesus!

It did *not* do the trick. She remained there on her wet backside, just as before. Unease nagged her consciousness, turning into a rising howl as she glanced down at her hand covered with dirt and her own dried blood. Before she could make another attempt to wake from her curious dream, she heard the snapping of branches and could see the brush ahead separating. Something was making its way through the undergrowth, pointed in her direction.

Maggie had never seen a bear before in real life, so it was a bit of a shock to see how immense the creature looked in her dream. Ah, okay! If she was trapped like a dirty little pig in an insufferable dream, she might as well get to see a bear up close! She smiled at her predicament and hoped she would remember it when she woke up.

Walking on all fours, the massive bear was a solid chunk of dense brown fur. He lumbered toward her in a lazy swagger, his enormous head swinging back and forth. The creature's head stopped abruptly when his deep brown eyes swung her way, and his weight shifted somewhat backward on his haunches, although he did not actually sit down.

Maggie stuck her dirty palm up and waved, as if the bear was sitting behind a fence at the zoo.

"Hey...bear," she whispered. It seemed odd that she could feel the dampness through her denim jeans as she rolled forward onto her knees. She was fine with ignoring that bit of information, much more focused on getting close to the animal in her dream. As she reached for him, the beast opened its mouth and uttered a snarl, and she scrunched her nose. Rancid breath, indeed!

The beast rose upward on his hind legs, still roaring his displeasure, his front limbs extended outward so close to her head she could see the round pink pads on the underside of his paws. She pushed off with her feet and scrambled backward on her bottom, then turned over to crawl away faster. Dream or no dream, she did not want to be eaten by a wild animal.

Didn't someone once say if you died in a dream, you died in real life?

She was not willing to test the theory. She was still considering that idea when she felt the blow to her right shoulder followed by a searing pain as she was slammed flat to the ground, the air from her lungs evacuating in one painful rush. Her mouth again tasted the dirt as she struggled to gasp for air.

"*Ikali-a!*" A shrill voice whooped from very near her face. Maggie could not see with her cheek pressed down into the ground, but she felt the air above her swoosh and the weight of the massive paw was suddenly gone from her back. The bear sounded angrier at the intrusion, his roaring mingled with the sharp rapid cries coming from what sounded like a man. Maggie pulled at the ground with her broken fingernails and struggled to breathe but her crushed ribs refused to expand. She managed to curl into a half sitting position and backed away from the melee at her feet. Her shoulder screamed in protest with every move and a steady trickle of blood dripped down the front of her parka.

The scene in front of her was very much like a movie - the brown bear stood on his hind legs, his front paws extended outward, looking as if he were about to give the man standing in front of him a hug. Only the bear was truly, really, there in front of her. Moreover, crouched between her and the bear was a tan-skinned man, lithe and quick on his toes, wielding what looked like a rather small knife in consideration of the size of his opponent.

"*Ikali-a nusheaxkw!*" the man roared, as if in challenge to the beast.

The stranger danced away from a swipe by the bear, eliciting another frustrated bellow from the beast. Maggie could see the muscles of his legs flex through the buckskin leggings he wore, and there were colored beads attached to a belt at his waist that bounced when he jumped. She had not gained enough breath back in her lungs yet to scream, but if she had, she would have been screaming by now from the absurdity of it all.

The bear aimed another seeming half-hearted swipe at the man, and then gave his massive head a shake as he dropped back down on all fours. The man remained crouched between her and the beast, his fist extended with the knife pointing at it, the veins on his muscled arms standing out like cords against his skin. With one last series of groans and roars, the animal tossed his head and then abruptly swung his shoulder

244

around. The beast lumbered back the way it came through the underbrush. It appeared to have lost interest in the fight.

The man watched the bear retreat. When he was satisfied the animal was gone, the stranger turned to Maggie. She could see beads of sweat sliding down off his brow along his black hair. There was a thin braid down the left side of his face where his hair laid flat just past his bare brown shoulders, but she was perplexed to notice the right side of his head was shaved clean in a crescent shape from temple to nape. She could see the bone-handled knife he still clutched in his hand as he glared at her. His hands were fisted at his sides and his chest heaved with the effort of slowing down his breathing. Maggie was too stunned to speak, but even just staring at him in return of his sharpened gaze was too much. She felt her head spinning as if she would vomit, but the last thing she wanted to do was throw up in front of the stranger, so she leaned forward and put her head in her hands.

"*Keptchat!*"

She heard the utterance that sounded like a curse, and felt his presence when he kneeled down beside her. Uncontrolled shaking coursed through her and she felt she was going to lose her head to a moment of panic. None of it made any sense. The warm hands on her upper arms sent a shock through her bones, and the man holding her was most certainly *not* a dream.

Everything that had just happened was real.

The man muttered words she did not understand, as if talking to himself in another language. Maggie felt fingers grasp her chin and then the wet rim of some sort of container of water as he pressed it to her lips. She took a few sips and then shook her head to show him she had enough.

"*Aptamehele,*" he muttered.

He sat back on his haunches in front of her, now an unmoving statue as he surveyed her. Maggie returned his bold gaze this time. She imagined she should feel uncomfortable with the way his eyes raked over her, but she did the same to him so she figured they were on equal footing. Other than his brown buckskin leggings and knotted rawhide beaded belt, he was adorned with rawhide ties above each bicep and a pendant necklace decorated with beads and two black feathers. The necklace hung down his broad chest, banging against his caramel skin when he moved. Some sort of hanging flap was secured around his hips by a narrow cord...was it a breechcloth?

His features could not be called handsome by the standards she was accustomed, but there was a fierce strength in the sharp lines of his face that captivated her. When she slowly returned her gaze back to his eyes, she was startled to find they were a luminous deep blue, which seemed peculiar for an Indian. A corner of his mouth slanted downward as he met her appraisal with his own.

"Why are you here, stupid woman?" he asked in clear, but hesitant English. She did not care for the mocking tone of his voice nor the way he raised his eyebrows to wait for her answer, as if he held some authority over her.

"I—I don't know," she managed to stammer. "Why are you here?" she countered. This was apparently a humorous response, and it caused him to laugh aloud and smile.

"Maybe you should be glad I am here. Lucky for you that bear was not too hungry."

Maggie closed her eyes and shook her head. Yup. Still there when opened her eyes and looked again. The blasted man was grinning as though she had provided him endless entertainment. How on Earth was she sitting in the middle of the woods after being attacked by a bear, with a man dressed in an Indian costume laughing at her? Maybe she had been sleepwalking and stumbled onto...onto what? Wait, Halloween was next month! Yes, that had to be it! An early Halloween party and some adults running around in the woods in costumes, perhaps taking things a little too seriously. Hell, the guy was probably drunk, especially considering the way he shaved the side of his head for one silly costume event!

She could think of no other explanation that made sense. She knew she was missing something important, but her brain seemed to be in a fog and the self-preservation of denial was controlling her senses.

"I really don't know how I got here, mister, but—"

Maggie snapped her mouth closed when remnants of memory began to rush back. She could recall picking up stones in the barn, and then cutting her hand.

The air surged like an electric charge as she looked down at the ground and the fine hair on her arms pricked up when she focused on the object. Lying on pine needles beside her was the dark green stone.

She slowly reached out and picked it up, its weight not too heavy but definitely substantial as she raised it in front of her face. It was still stained with her blood.

The man dropped to his knees beside her and snatched her wrist in his own large hand. His startling blue eyes widened and he drew back somewhat as he slowly raised his gaze to meet her own. She tried half-heartedly to pull her hand away, but he held it firm as his eyes remained locked with hers, a flutter settling down deep in her belly at the connection. She could see him swallow hard and his lips closed together in a tight line. Finally he spoke in a low, even tone, but his eyes remained fixed on her own.

"*Sawwehone Shacquohocan*," he said. "This is a Bloodstone. How did you come by it?"

"I found it in my barn. I was cleaning up. I dropped it, I guess," she stammered. Her answer was an honest one, but it seemed to incite his agitation.

"You say you found it? Or stole it?" he asked.

"No! I didn't *steal* it! I just found it," she tried to explain. "But I didn't steal it. It's just a *rock*, for Christ's sake!" she insisted. She had no idea why she was trying to justify herself to him. Despite the fact that she still felt disoriented and had been nearly mauled to death by a wild animal, she felt like she had to make him understand.

He plucked the stone from her hand and a hiss escaped from between his clenched teeth when they both saw the burn on her palm. A twist of lines scarred her skin where she held the stone, tender to touch and disturbingly...organized. As if a strange knot shape had been branded to her skin.

There was no more time to ponder her predicament because the man swiftly scooped her up and stood to his feet, holding her in his bare arms as if she weighed nothing at all. One hand rested gingerly around her shoulder where the bear had scratched her, and it was only then that she began to feel the sharp burning ache the claws had left in her skin.

"I can walk just fine, thank you," she protested. He glanced down at her.

"Your wound needs to be bound. You have lost much blood."

His purposeful gait cut a path through the underbrush, the tall growth brushing against his buckskin leggings as he navigated to a nearby clearing. When they entered the clearing where a sorrel horse stood patiently ground tied, he let Maggie's legs drop down but still he held his arms around her waist and kept her close. Her chin was even with his collarbone, and her cheek brushed against his chest when he refused to release her. The scent of sweat mixed with evergreen and smoke bonded to him, his skin slick with the heady combination. With a sickly feeling in her bones, Maggie glanced around the clearing. A panic began to rise as she looked at her surroundings and realized they were familiar.

They were standing at the entrance to her barn. Only it was not there.

She was aware it was damn impossible, but she knew the farm better than anyone did. They were standing on it—on her property. Two tall ancient Cyprus trees marked the spot behind the barn, overlooking a steep drop off that tumbled down to the river below. There was a winding gravel trail to navigate the slope, which still appeared to be there. She could hear the roar of the waterfall beyond the clearing.

The trees were shorter than they had been earlier in the day, the trunks a smaller diameter and their branches not yet as full. A split rail fence had guarded the drop off to the river below, but it was not anywhere to be seen now. Her fingers curled into fists and she barely felt it when her nails dug crescent-shaped daggers into her palms.

"You said you found the Bloodstone. When did you find it?"

She knew it made no sense, but the truth was the only thing she could cling to with any certainty in the midst of rising panic.

"I found it today. This morning, the fifth of October."

At this confession, he placed his fingers on her chin and twisted her head gently upwards to meet his stare, his head cocked to the side. His brows furrowed and his eyes searched her own in a question he could not seem to put to words. She did not understand what she was doing there, or who this man was. She was willing to wager he was just as confused as she was.

"It is now the month your people call September," he replied.

"But it can't be September," she insisted. "That doesn't make any sense! I was just here today, and I cut my hand— I think I passed out."

He touched her cheek gently with his thumb, shaking his head.

"This is the place I buried the Bloodstones one year ago. The ground is not disturbed. No one knows this place but me."

"What...what year did you bury them?" she whispered, the words rushing out before she could stop the ridiculous question.

"The year your people call 1621."

She felt relieved that his arms still held her as her knees buckled and the blessed darkness swallowed her one more time.

~ end preview ~

<u>Continue reading for free HERE ON AMAZON</u>

ABOUT THE AUTHOR

E.B. Brown enjoys researching history and genealogy and uses her findings to cultivate new ideas for her writing. Her debut novel, *The Legend of the Bloodstone* (Time Walkers #1), was a Quarter-finalist in the 2013 ABNA contest. An excerpt from another Time Walkers novel, *A Tale of Oak and Mistletoe* (Time Walkers #4), was a finalist in the 2013 RWA/NYC We Need a Hero Contest. She is also the author of the thriller novel *Jack Made Me Do It* written under the pen name Ellis Brown.

E.B. loves mudding in her Jeep Wrangler and likes to cause all kinds of havoc the rest of the time. She resides in New Jersey.

Don't miss a thing!
Sign up for the VIP List
New Releases ~ VIP Discounts ~ E.B. Brown news

Prefer Amazon updates?

CLICK HERE TO FOLLOW E.B. BROWN ON AUTHOR CENTRAL & GET NOTIFIED WHEN NEW BOOKS ARE RELEASED.

CONNECT WITH ME ONLINE

TWITTER: www.twitter.com/ebbrown_

FACEBOOK: www.facebook.com/ebbrownauthor

GOODREADS: www.goodreads.com/EBBrown

BOOKS BY E.B. BROWN

TIME WALKERS

The Legend of the Bloodstone

Return of the Pale Feather

Of Vice and Virtue

A Tale of Oak and Mistletoe

Time Walkers The Complete Collection

TIME WALKERS: TIME SONG

THE PRETENDERS

The Seventh Key

The Fifth Key

The Ninth Key

The Pretenders Complete Collection

TIME DANCE

Ghost Dance

Season of Exile

TIME WALKERS WORLD

Roam: Time Walkers World Special Edition

THE ARRANGEMENT: THE REPLACEMENT

The Replacement Part 1

The Replacement Part 2

The Replacement Part 3

THE CHRONOS FILES: THE VIKING SAGAS

Time Rift

Time Game

Time Over

The Viking Sagas Collection

WRITING AS ELLIS BROWN

Jack Made Me Do It

Made in the USA
Middletown, DE
19 June 2017